"I was not chasing you! And I haven't the faintest idea what you're talking about!"

"Haven't you? Do you not consider that I might be curious to see if there is anything inside you worth the love that Umberto and your mother lavish on you?"

"What?" Rea gasped.

"It's what you want—to be kissed. By me."

"No! You think I want to be kissed as a punishment?"

"Then how *do* you want to be kissed?" Tano asked softly.

Dear Reader,

Welcome to the latest book in our **Holding Out for A Hero** series. Every month for a whole year we'll be bringing you some of the world's most eligible men. They're handsome, they're charming but, best of all, they're single! And as twelve lucky women are about to discover, it's not finding Mr. Right that's the problem—it's holding on to him!

Hold out for Harlequin Romance's heroes in coming months....

Look out in November for:

Bringing Up Babies
by
Emma Goldrick

Happy reading!

The Editors
Harlequin Romance

Some men are worth waiting for!

The Bachelor Chase
Emma Richmond

Harlequin Books

TORONTO • NEW YORK • LONDON
AMSTERDAM • PARIS • SYDNEY • HAMBURG
STOCKHOLM • ATHENS • TOKYO • MILAN
MADRID • WARSAW • BUDAPEST • AUCKLAND

ISBN 0-373-03430-X

THE BACHELOR CHASE

First North American Publication 1996.

Printed in U.S.A.

CHAPTER ONE

'AND if I never see another basilisk or obelisk, or whatever they're blasted well called, it will be far too soon! I don't care *who* they have on top!' No, that wasn't fair, but worry over her own problems, *and* the pouring rain, had taken away any enjoyment she might otherwise have felt. And Rome did have rather a *lot* of statues!

Shoving back her wet hair, tiredly slinging her bag onto the chair, Rea came to an abrupt halt, and her insides produced that familiar low spiral of pain as she stared at the man sprawled on the sofa. Tano Cavallieri.

There was rather a lot of him to stare at. Long and lean—suave, sophisticated, impressive, her mind added—he was the most infuriating, aggravating man she'd ever met. And the most attractive. He was also the root cause of all her irritability and frustration.

She had been falling over him for weeks—well, four days, she mentally qualified, but it felt like weeks. And if it wasn't him it was a box of his filthy rocks, or bones, or some other rubbish he'd dug up.

And why he had to come and stay in her step-father's apartment instead of using his own defied her comprehension. There wasn't *room* for him here! Never mind heavy hints, he didn't take any notice of blunt speaking! He took no notice whatsoever of what was said and ignored all commands to keep his rubbish in one place—none of which would have mattered if they'd been friends. But they weren't friends, and her shrewish behaviour—her defence against feelings she didn't want or know how to cope with—guaranteed that they never would be.

And he *still* hadn't had time to talk to her! Or so he said. Another bone of contention, this refusal of his to put aside his own concerns for just a few minutes in order to discuss hers. She knew he was busy, but then, so was she.

Her face mirroring her confused aggravation, she continued to stare at him, at that sternly beautiful face emphasised so starkly by the ruthlessly short dark hair, at the stupid bone held loosely in one hand— and she wanted to touch him, to trail her fingers along that hard jaw, his mouth. Wanted to be held, touched, aroused.

Then she gave a little jump of alarm when he suddenly opened his eyes. Embarrassed, defensive, she went immediately on the attack.

'Do you *have* to spread yourself all over the lounge?' Ignoring for the moment the fact that there had been no confusion in his gaze, which was what normally appeared when you woke someone suddenly, and the odd contradiction that in sleep his face had seemed harder than when he was awake, she snapped peevishly, 'If you're that tired, go to bed! The lounge isn't for sleeping in!'

Derisive amusement leached into his grey eyes, and she felt goaded—almost violent. Amused grey eyes didn't go with a stern face! They were a complete and utter contradiction. 'Well? What are you waiting for— the spell to work?'

'Spell?'

Pointing at the bone he still held, Rea qualified with pardonable sarcasm, 'Practising to be a shaman, are we?'

He didn't blink, didn't change expression at all, merely continued to regard her with hateful consideration. 'Dear lady,' he drawled softly, 'if I were capable of spell-casting . . .'

'You would get rid of me—yes, I know. Well, you were the one who insisted I come!' He had sent a terse letter demanding her attendance and an air ticket, and she'd had no choice, wanting everything resolved as she did. 'Four days I've been here. I don't have *time* for this.'

'No more do I.'

'Then let me have the land.'

'No,' he refused quietly. 'What time is it?'

'One! And I—'

'*One*? You're very late tonight.'

'So?' she demanded, with a frosty look. 'Since when have you been my keeper?'

Eyebrows raised in surprise, he drew in his legs, lounged more comfortably, and absently began to revolve the bone between his long fingers. 'That sounded very defensive. Been cheating on Spindleshanks?'

'No,' she denied stonily. The reason she was so late was that she'd had to walk home because she'd given her cab fare, and her umbrella, to an elderly lady who'd been wetter and more tired than she had.

'Pity; it would do you the world of good. How is he, by the way? Still intending to marry you?'

'Presumably,' she agreed shortly. 'And as far as I know he's fine. How's Desirée?'

With a look of astonishment, he demanded. 'Who?'

'Desirée.'

'Sounds like a snake-wielding stripper.'

'Which for all I know she is,' she retorted tartly. 'Desdemona, then. Or something. Some outlandish name anyway.' And, reverting to the one topic that was of any interest to her—*had* to be of any interest to her—she stated flatly, 'You don't *know* there's a Pict settlement there.'

'I do.'

'No, you don't. Only suspect. And I wish you'd get up!'

He smiled without warmth, pressed his hands to his knees and levered himself upright, all six feet four of him. 'Better?' he asked mockingly.

'Yes.' Only it wasn't. Turning away, she caught a glimpse of her reflection in the ornate mirror over the mantelpiece, and wanted to weep. She looked like a bad-tempered shrew—brown eyes hard, too bright, her face pinched. And she wasn't like that. She also looked Egyptian or Italian—and was as English as roast beef.

With her thick, straight dark brown hair parted in the middle and drawn loosely back at her nape, she could have posed for Leonardo. Only the enigmatic smile was missing. But enigma and Rea weren't even nodding acquaintances.

And she hated it—this feeling of being out of control, of sounding shrewish. But, if he wasn't to guess how she felt, there seemed no choice. Indifference would have been better, but these churning feelings inside her didn't allow for indifference.

Aware that he'd gone to lean in the doorway, she raised her eyes to stare at him. Tano—the man she was cheating, the man who didn't know she was cheating, the man who disturbed her so much that she thought she'd go mad, the man who wouldn't let her have the piece of land she so desperately needed. And it wasn't meant to be like this!

He looked like a Regency rake, she thought despondently, and spoke like one—when he used English, that was. She didn't know how he sounded when he spoke his native Italian; the same, presumably—an upper-class drawl that made him sound like an aristocrat. That was his mother's fault, her stepfather always insisted, for sending him to an English public school.

'What time are Umberto and your mother due back?' he asked casually.

'I don't know,' she said moodily. 'Soon, I expect.' Tucking her thick brown hair behind her ears with a gesture of weariness, *knowing* that she was battering her head against a brick wall, she nevertheless tried again. 'And even if there does turn out to be a Pict settlement there, couldn't I rent it short-term until you're ready to dig?' she pleaded.

'No,' he refused softly.

'But *why*? I don't want to work the land—won't disturb anything! All I want is to put up a few sheds!'

'No.'

Impotent and frustrated, not knowing how to make him change his mind, she just continued to stare helplessly at him. He was a world authority on antiquities and his shirt looked as though it had never even *heard* of an iron, let alone come anywhere near one.

His trousers were no better. One pocket was torn, there was a smear of mud along the inside of one leg, and his shoes were filthy. Fieldwork, she supposed vaguely. He might be head of the newly formed European Historical Preservation Society but he never minded getting his hands dirty—a point in his favour, she supposed.

He looked different through the mirror—his nose more blade-like, his mouth thinner. And she saw that his attention had wandered back into the past, presumably, as it often wandered.

Only a very small portion of his mind was ever on anything in the present. Or so it seemed. He listened with half an ear, answered with half a mind, and it was totally infuriating. If you ever did manage to capture his attention, you had to speak very quickly in order to get everything in before his mind wandered off again. And yet she sometimes got the feeling that he was being vague on purpose—and only with her. But that didn't make any sense.

He also looked like the statue of Hadrian's favourite, Antinous, she thought inconsequentially as she continued to stare frowningly at him. He looked . . . unreachable, apart from his eyes—and it was his eyes that had persuaded her that he would understand, and he didn't. If he had, he would have let her use the land. Abominably selfish, single-minded, clever and calculating, he didn't give a damn about anybody's feelings but his own. Just like herself, she thought miserably.

Worry lines etched on her brow, so very aware that time was running out, she looked down. She *needed* that land. *Really* needed it. And, if he wouldn't give in, what on earth was she going to do?

'Did Mike Resnick ring?' she asked quietly. Receiving no answer, she looked up to find him gone. Sighing deeply, utterly refusing to give in to feelings she didn't want, she walked along to his room and pushed the door wide.

He was sitting on the edge of his bed, staring at the floor, or his shoes. Perhaps he was trying to figure out how they'd got so dirty, but she wouldn't have bet on it. 'I do wish you wouldn't walk off when I'm talking to you,' she reproved tiredly. 'I asked if you'd spoken to Mike Resni—Tano!'

'Mmm?' Glancing up, he waited, then began absently to unbutton his shirt.

Wrenching her eyes away from the expanse of naked chest—a chest she wanted to touch, caress—she repeated huskily, 'Resnick! Has he got the aerial photographs back?'

'Mmm.'

'And?'

Abandoning his shirt, he began thoughtfully to tap one fingernail against the bone. 'Too early to tell,' he murmured.

'What does that mean? That there's no sign of a Pict settlement? Or there is?'

Eyes unfocused, he glanced up. 'Too high.'

'High?' she queried in puzzlement. 'What's too high? Tano!' Oh, for goodness' sake! Taking a deep breath, trying desperately to hang onto her scant patience and to dismiss desire, she cleared her throat, then asked quietly, 'Do you mean that the photographs were taken from too high up? And, that being so,' she continued, her voice beginning to grit, 'will he be taking some more from lower down?'

'Mmm.'

'When? Tomorrow? The next day? And if *those* don't show anything can I then rent the land?'

'No, there's *something*,' he mumbled to himself, a small frown of concentration on his face. 'But what? Could be fake; could be any number of reasons—'

'Tano!' She didn't even know if they were talking about the same things, didn't know if he was listening or even aware that she was there! 'Will you please pay attention? This is important!'

He gave a vague nod, and continued to unbutton his shirt.

Taking that to mean that he *was* actually listening, she continued eagerly, 'If you could just give me the go-ahead, an agreement on a week to week basis— *anything*—I can get things moving.'

Staring at him, silently urging him to agree, she held her tongue with difficulty as he heeled off his shoes, removed his socks and began absentmindedly rolling them together. Unaware of her, unaware of anything but his thoughts, he pitched them into the corner.

'Don't do that,' she reproved automatically as she went to pick them up and drop them in the laundry basket. 'My mother has enough to do without picking up after you! So when will you know?' she persisted.

'Soon,' he said vaguely. 'Umberto might know.'

'Umberto might know what?'

'Augustus—it's his period.'

'*Augustus*? Augustus!' she practically screeched. 'We aren't talking about Augustus! We're talking about a Pict settlement in Kent!'

Without warning, without any advance notice whatsoever, he suddenly glanced up, gave her a look of surprise, as though he had no memory of having been holding a conversation with her—and certainly not of what it had been about—and stated, 'Your mother seems very contented with her new life.'

'What? What's that got to do with anything?'

'Don't you like Umberto?'

'Of course I like Umberto!' she snapped raggedly. 'He's a sweetie, the best thing that could ever have happened to her. But we were—'

'She was widowed when you were three, wasn't she?'

'Yes, but—'

'That accounts for it,' he murmured.

'Accounts for what?' she demanded aggrievedly. 'I'm delighted at the match, all right? Umberto's brought a bloom to her cheeks, a sparkle to her eyes. He's a good man, kind...' And so undeniably proud and happy.

He had never been married before, and now couldn't seem to get over the fact that Jean Halton was his wife, loving him in return. Shorter than Rea's mother, round and balding, he seemed afraid that someone would snatch it all away, and if he was a little bit protective of mother and daughter both forgave him his fussing because they understood.

And none of this had anything to do with the matter in hand—the matter that she *had* to get resolved.

'So can I? Rent it on a day-to-day basis? And then, when Mike's taken the rest of the photographs, you'll let me know for definite? Yes?'

'Perhaps,' he agreed.

'Perhaps you'll let me know? Or perhaps you'll agree?' If you didn't qualify every wretched utterance you ended up in more of a muddle than when you started. 'I—' Hearing a key in the lock, she broke off. Frustrated, she closed her eyes in defeat and turned to watch the front door open.

'Rea?' her mother called softly, and then smiled when she saw her daughter. 'Everything all right?'

'Yes, fine.'

'Tour go all right?'

'Fine,' she agreed again. Remembering her irritated thoughts when she'd come in, she gave a somewhat sour smile, and then rather overdid her enthusiasm to make up for the fact that her mind hadn't been on what she'd been seeing, that ancient Rome had passed her in something of a blur. 'I learned all about Bernini, and aqueducts, the Trinità dei Monti, the—er—Fountain of the Barcaccia, and the Spanish Steps.'

'You've eaten?'

'Yes, at Da Piperno.'

'Good.' Her mother smiled. 'And you enjoyed it?'

'Yes. Very much.'

Not looking totally satisfied, the older woman nodded. 'Gaetano is in?' she added, with a smile that was just a little too hopeful.

'Yes. And I was merely in his room,' Rea explained pointedly, 'to ask him something.'

'About the land, yes,' her mother agreed, with a disappointed sigh.

'You must be the only mother in the world who yearns for her daughter to leap into a man's bed unwed!'

'I do not!' she denied emphatically. Too emphatically. 'And I shouldn't think a man would want you in his bed the way you've been dressing lately.'

Totally astonished, Rea glanced down at herself. 'What's wrong with the way I look? I'm only wearing jeans.'

'Precisely. Men like to see *legs.*'

'Rubbish. Anyway, I didn't pack anything smart. I didn't come to socialise. Or to attract a man to my bed.'

'I know,' her mother sighed. Abandoning her daughter as a lost cause, she peeped into the bedroom and gave Tano a sheepish smile. Rea didn't bother to look to see whether he returned it.

And, as though he were deaf, which he emphatically was not, and couldn't possibly have heard the preceding conversation, Umberto called anxiously from behind his wife, 'Rea is in?'

His head appeared over her mother's shoulder, his expression a mixture of worry, pride and sheer dumbfounded bewilderment at his luck that, at the age of fifty-two, he had found not only a lovely new wife but a beautiful daughter as well—and overwhelming love. He beamed at Rea and announced unnecessarily, 'We are in.'

'So I see,' she agreed, then gave him a quick smile to show that her aggravation wasn't with him, and then gave a gentler one because his feelings could be so easily hurt. She did love him, and doubted if she could have loved him more if he'd been her real father.

He returned her smile with a lovely twinkle in his eyes, then turned to look into the bedroom. '*Buonasera*, Gaetano,' he greeted, and for a moment worriedly surveyed Gaetano's bare chest and feet. 'Is all right?'

'Meaning, should your daughter be in my bedroom?' Gaetano asked, with his hatefully mocking smile. 'No, she shouldn't. But it's all right,' he reassured, 'I haven't been trying to ravish her.'

'As if you could,' Rea muttered. But he *could*, she thought with a return to despondency, because she *wanted* him to—and she suspected that he knew it.

'I know this!' Umberto exclaimed. 'Is not what I meant.'

'You *want* me to ravish her?'

'No!'

'I mean, I can quite understand that you might not want a twenty-nine-year-old spinster cluttering up your life, and old Spindleshanks does seem to be taking his time about—'

'Gaetano!' her mother reproved. 'You shouldn't call him that! I'm sure Tom is very nice—once you get to know him,' she concluded a little uncertainly.

'And you don't know him yet? After—what—two years?'

'Eighteen months,' Rea put in, sweetly helpful, wishing they would all shut up. 'About the length of time you've been going out with your stripper.'

'Stripper?' her mother exclaimed in horror. 'Oh, Gaetano, no—not a stripper!'

'With snake,' Rea put in even more helpfully. 'Python, I think.'

'Viper,' he murmured.

Surprised by the dry humour—not something she would have associated with him—she glanced quickly away when he looked at her, that derisive amusement back in his eyes.

If only she knew what sort of person he was she thought helplessly; it would be easier to know how to act. But she didn't know. Didn't understand him at all! One minute he was almost friendly, and the next he'd withdrawn, leaving only a cold outer shell, his thoughts hidden from everyone but himself. He was intimidating, and even mud-stained clothes could not hide that air of sophistication, that aura of importance.

'Viper?' her mother queried weakly as she stared from one to the other, then gave a moue of exasperation. 'Oh, I'm going to bed.'

She pushed Umberto out with her backside and they moved along the hall to their own room. Rea could hear the quiet murmur of their conversation. Probably trying to convince themselves that she liked Gaetano after all, she thought, but then her mother lived most of her life in cloud-cuckoo-land—thought everyone should like everyone—and she *didn't* like Gaetano— was only affected by him.

If he would only forgo his interest in the land she could go away, try to forget. She hadn't expected that he would refuse her, had assumed . . . altogether too much. But if she left without his agreement . . .

Glancing at him, only to find that he was watching her, an expression of amused knowledge on his face, she gave him a sour look.

'Never mind, Rea,' he comforted. 'Think of it as character-building. Setbacks *always* build character.'

'For good or ill?' she asked tartly.

'Ah, that is the question.' Rising, with that hateful smile still playing about his mouth, he prodded her backwards. 'And your mother was right,' he added provokingly. 'Men do like to see legs.' Before she could answer, react, he closed the door gently but firmly in her face.

'How would you know?' she queried irritably, but too low for him to hear. 'If it isn't two thousand years old you don't even *see* it! I'll talk to you in the morning!' she added loudly.

'Don't bother,' he returned, his own voice barely audible through the wooden panels. 'The answer will still be no.'

'But why?' she wailed. When there was no further communication she trailed along to her own room. 'Why?' she demanded of her empty room. What possible difference could it make to him?

Well, she wasn't going to give up—*couldn't* give up—and, hopefully, eventually he would get so fed up with her that he would agree, just to get her out of his hair! Only, if it wasn't soon he would find out what she had done—and then all hell would break loose.

Thankfully kicking off her shoes, she sat on the edge of the bed to massage her aching feet. And tomorrow she had promised Umberto that she would view the Vatican and ancient monuments. She knew that he was yearning for her to love his city as he did, yearning for her to move out to Rome so that they could all be together. She sighed. She loved him dearly, but love put such a responsibility on the one who was loved.

With a faint smile, then a frown as she remembered the conversation with Gaetano—well, half-conversation—she'd conversed and he'd looked vague—she sent up another little prayer that he would change his mind. Then she could go home, get her life back on an even keel again. And go back to Tom, she thought, with another sigh—Tom, who wanted to marry her. But she wasn't in love with him. He was another arrogant male who thought he only had to proclaim something for it to be so.

But she did miss her animals, and if Tano had never come into her life... If he wouldn't agree to rent her the land, there would be no animals to go back to—no wildlife shelter, no kennels, the bank loan revoked, and all her plans, hopes and dreams, in ashes. And all because Tano wouldn't make up his mind about the field.

Ralph Bressingham, the farmer she *had* rented some land from, had died, and his brother, who'd inherited, had sold it out from under her—because she had stupidly not insisted on a proper lease, because she had not expected Ralph to die. Nor had Ralph, presumably. He'd only been in his early fifties.

But she'd *accepted* that! She'd found another piece of land less than a mile away, near enough for people to be able to find her easily... And if Umberto hadn't shown Tano the land... If Tano hadn't seen something that had led him to believe in the Pict settlement... If, if, if, she thought despondently. She sometimes wondered if there wasn't a malicious God up there, causing trouble.

Getting up wearily, she went to get ready for bed, and when she was lying under the duvet, hands beneath her head, staring at the ceiling, her mind, without any prompting, reverted to Tano— Tano who was lying a few feet away in another bed, his long, lean, hard body naked, perhaps . . .

With a low groan, frustration and longing making her ache, she clenched her hands into fists and fought to dismiss him. It was crazy, so crazy, for her body to yearn in this ridiculous way—especially as he thought of her as a dried-up old spinster. Well, no, that wasn't exactly what he'd said . . . only implied.

With a deep sigh, forcing herself to dismiss it— him—she focused on her own life, her own beliefs. She'd have to get back soon, with or without Tano's consent to use the land; she couldn't leave her assistant, Lucy, to cope with things too long on her own. But the piece of land was so *perfect*.

And then there was Tom with his ultimatum—in effect, Marry me or else. And she'd told him and *told* him that she wasn't in love with him, only liked him as a friend—but had he listened? No. She didn't think he'd even understood her. He'd fallen in love with her looks, not the person, and was now doggedly sticking to feelings he thought he had. Lucy would have suited him far better.

And there you go again, Rea, thinking you know best! But she wasn't in love with him. Perhaps she wasn't the loving kind. Perhaps she was too picky. The trouble was that she was too independent, and men didn't seem to like that. They didn't like her dashing off in the middle of the night to rescue sick wildlife either.

Certainly Tom hadn't liked it, even though he'd known when he'd first met her that that was what she did. Tom was the local vet, who didn't seem to like animals as *animals*, only, she thought rather cynically, as a source of revenue. And yet he would always trundle out to look at her sick foxes and hedgehogs, and being married to a vet would certainly be handy... Oh, Rea, now who's being cynical? Although being a direct antithesis of Gaetano *should* have been in Tom's favour.

How her mother had ever thought she and Tano would make a pair, she had no idea! Tano had made it perfectly obvious that he didn't like her! But then, as she had often thought before, women in love seemed to view everything in the whole world through rose-coloured spectacles—even muck heaps!

Even Umberto was at it. He would be delighted if she fell in love with his very good friend—or some other Italian—just so that she would stay in her mother's adopted land.

And why Tano had insisted that she come out when he wouldn't even *discuss* the land, she had no idea. She had rushed out in hope, wrongly assuming that he might have changed his mind, would thrash out details of a lease ... So why *had* he insisted she come?

With a bewildered sigh she rolled over and closed her eyes. She'd have one last try tomorrow, and then if she had no joy she'd have to go home, look for something else. But there wasn't anything else, she thought worriedly. She'd already looked!

Waking late, she stared blankly at the bedside clock for a moment, then groaned. Nine o'clock, which meant that she'd probably missed Tano again, and it was no good searching him out at his dig because she knew that he wouldn't talk to her there. And she'd promised Umberto to tour Rome—and why didn't someone answer that wretched phone?

When it continued to ring she hauled herself out of bed, stumbled into the hall—and it stopped. Cursing, about to wander along to the kitchen for a cup of coffee, she saw the letter addressed to her tucked under the directory—Lucy's dreadful handwriting scrawled across the envelope.

Tearing it open, the name Bressingham leapt out at her and she felt a little surge of hope. Perhaps he'd changed his mind, was going to allow her to rent the land after all. She could move everything back there before Tano found out...

Quickly scanning it, her expression of hope changed rapidly to despair. He was going to *what*? she thought in disbelief. *Charge* her? He couldn't do that! Couldn't charge her for restoring the land to its former use. That was crazy! He was going to build on it, for goodness' sake; it didn't matter what state the land was in! Well, she wasn't going to pay it! she determined. Let him take her to court! Let him *sue* her! He'd already taken everything else there was to take!

Pushing into the dining room, she came to a lame halt. Tano was there, coffee-cup in one hand, his nose buried in a book, papers spread all over the highly polished table. Every time she saw him that same spiral went through her, that utter *yearning*.

You'd think her stupid body would get used to him after four days of proximity. *Look* at me, she wanted to shout. See me as I am! But he wouldn't; she knew he wouldn't, and so that restless aggravation surfaced—behaviour that made her a stranger even to herself.

He glanced up, glanced at her nightie, and returned his attention to his book.

Feeling diminished, she slumped down opposite him. 'Have you spoken to Resnick?'

He gave a slight shake of his head.

'Why not? And I wish you'd look at me when I'm talking to you.' Reaching out, she lowered the book away from his nose. 'I got a letter.'

'So I see.'

Ignoring his indifference, she stated, 'Bressingham says I have to pay to restore the land to its former glory—which is absolute rubbish; it didn't have any glory! Can he do that?'

He stared at her briefly, looked annoyed, then returned to his indifference. 'I've no idea. I'm not a lawyer.'

'I know you aren't a lawyer, but you have land—'

'Which I can't allow you to use.'

'But *why*?' she pleaded. 'And, if he's going to sue, there's even *more* need! I'll need the revenue from the kennels—'

'Counter-sue,' he murmured as he returned his attention to his book. 'Refuse to move from the land.'

I've already moved from the land! Onto yours. Only how could she tell him? If he would only agree, he need never know! 'Tano...'

'*Gae*tano,' he corrected.

Stifling a wail, she repeated obediently, 'Gaetano...'

'No.'

'No, what?'

'No, you can't have the land.'

'You said I could have it if there wasn't a settlement there!'

'*You* said. And it isn't *my* land. It belongs to the local council; we merely have an option in order to pursue historical research.'

'But you're in charge! You could persuade them! They'd listen to you! And I *need* it!'

Slowly putting down his cup, he rested the spine of the book against the table edge and looked at her. His face seemed incredibly cold, carved in marble. '*You* need it? Must everything revolve around you and your concerns? Is there no value in the fact that the land is of vital interest archaeologically? That so few sites remain? It is your *heritage*!'

'So are wild animals! And you can still dig it; you can dig round me. Damn it, Tano, this is important!'

'So is archaeology.'

'But you said yourself that you had no time to look into it now—'

'*I* don't, no. But there are other members of the team, and I have people looking for another site for you—'

'But none very near! I've looked, and the only plots of any use are too far away.'

'No,' he denied coldly, 'the only thing far away is your understanding. *You* want; *you* must have. I have expended a great deal of time, patience and diplomacy in persuading your local council and your Department of the Environment that an effort must be made to find you a suitable alternative—that your work is important. As a personal favour to me they are doing so.'

'But not in the right area!' she repeated. 'I know you're trying, and I *am* grateful, but I can't leave it any longer! I have to get back!'

Slamming his book down, he got to his feet, and in a voice of muted thunder that totally astonished her said, 'Go back. Today. I will even drive you to the airport. You accuse me of being selfish, or cluttering up the apartment; do you accuse yourself of hurting Umberto and your mother with your aggravations and disruptions?'

'I'm not hurting them,' she denied in bewilderment.

'Yes, you are. You cause dissension—upset the tranquillity of our days.'

' "Tranquillity"?' she echoed weakly.

'*Sì*, tranquillity. Umberto has gone out of his way to accommodate you, to make your stay enjoyable—'

'But I wouldn't have needed to stay if you'd let me have the land! Wouldn't have needed to come out at all!'

'No—a fact they know only too well.'

Taken aback, she gasped, 'What?'

'How many years would it have taken you, Rea, to come visit them? See where they live, how they live? Months? Years?'

'No! But I don't have much free time!'

He gave a mirthless smile. 'But you have time to go chasing me.'

'I'm not chasing you! You *insisted* I come!'

'Yes,' he agreed silkily, 'insisted. And if I had not you would never have done so. And how do you think that makes your mother feel? How does it make Umberto feel—that you came because of me, not them?'

'That's not fair!'

'Isn't it?'

'No, and just because you work for Umberto it doesn't give you the right to talk to me as though I'm a little nobody!'

'I do not work *for* Umberto,' he corrected her icily.

'Oh—well, it doesn't matter whether you do or you don't.' Feeling guilty and unsure, because his accusations had hit too close to home, she went on the defensive—just as she was *always* on the defensive with this man. 'And, if we're levelling accusations, what about your inattention, your selfish disregard for anyone's feelings but your own? Don't you think my mother *and* Umberto aren't sick to death of your bones, your rocks, your very presence in their home? And—'

'My home,' he put in quietly, for the moment unheard.

'—they've only been married six months! I was giving them time to be together, which is a great deal more than you've done! You're rude and insensitive, interfering in the life of a newly married couple—a dear couple, a couple who certainly don't need you filling their home with your rubbish! Mother can't even clean properly! She does your washing and ironing with no more than— Your home?' she broke off to whisper in shock. '*Your* home? What do you mean, your home?'

'Exactly what I say.' Leaning across the table, he collected up his papers, shoved them into the book, carefully closed it, tucked it beneath his arm, and walked out.

CHAPTER TWO

'TANO!'

Shocked, bewildered, thoroughly perplexed, Rea hurried after him just in time to see the front door close. *His* home?

Staring round her at the old paintings, the antique furniture, the exquisite carpets, she whirled around and went in frantic search of her mother. Checking her bedroom, the lounge, then finally the kitchen, she saw her out on the balcony, chatting to the woman next door. She loved all this balcony business, her mother. It was better than a garden fence. But it wasn't *her* fence.

Walking out onto the wide, wrought-iron structure that held not only a vine but numerous flowerpots, all with something or other growing in them, she said quietly, 'Mother, can I have a word with you please?'

Looking surprised, hastily excusing herself to her neighbour in her newly acquired Italian, she tutted at her daughter and ushered her back inside. 'Rea! You're still in your nightie!'

'I know I'm still in my nightie,' she agreed impatiently. 'I overslept—'

'And you promised Umberto that you would go and see the Vatican. I believe the guided tour starts at eleven.'

'I know, but—'

'And he'll be very upset if you—'

28

'Mother! Tano said that this is *his* apartment!'

'Well, yes,' she agreed in some bewilderment. 'I told you—'

'No, you didn't.'

'Rea,' her mother argued gently, 'I told you when we picked you up from the airport, and please don't talk to me as though I'm stupid.'

Eyes wide, Rea was about to make a vehement denial when her mother continued, 'Ever since you arrived—the very second you stepped into the arrivals lounge at the airport, in fact—you've been behaving as though everyone were your enemy—snapping, throwing your weight around, being abominably rude to Tano, who, if I may say so, has been remarkably restrained about it all—but enough is enough.

'I know you're worried about your animal shelter, about the animals, but it isn't my fault, or Tano's or Umberto's.

'And Tano doesn't have to rent you the land; it isn't your God-given right to have it and, much as it hurts me to admit it, I've been thoroughly ashamed of you. I didn't bring you up to behave in this disgraceful fashion, and, if that's what associating with Tom does to you, then the sooner the relationship ends, the better. I—'

'We don't have a relationship,' she interrupted.

'I haven't said anything until now,' the older woman continued determinedly, 'because . . . well, because I was embarrassed.'

Shocked, almost speechless, Rea whispered, 'Embarrassed?'

'Yes. Umberto's been telling everyone—*everyone*—what a wonderful new daughter he has. He's so proud, so happy, and you've barely acknowledged *anyone*—almost threw any offer he made to take you about and introduce you to his friends back in his teeth.'

'No!'

'Yes. I know it wasn't meant—that you were distracted, unthinking—but this is my home now. These are people I meet every day—and I don't want them to talk about my daughter behind my back, say what a shame it is that she's so—'

'Rude?' Rea choked.

'Forceful,' her mother put in. 'This isn't like you!' Pausing, she bit her lip, then sighed. 'Yes, it is,' she confessed. 'You are forceful, but you never used to be rude. People *matter*, Rea. You can't dismiss them because they don't interest you, or because your mind's on something else.

'I thought it would be so nice,' she added wistfully, 'to have my daughter here, show her off. But you wouldn't have come, would you, if it hadn't been for that wretched piece of land?'

Feeling dreadful, shocked, Rea argued faintly, 'Of course I would have come, but it's only been six months; I thought you'd want to be on your own.'

'Did you?'

'Yes.' But that wasn't entirely true; that was what she'd *told* herself as a sop to her conscience. The real truth was that she'd become so involved with her animal shelter that everything else had taken second place. She had *known* that Umberto and her mother had positively yearned to show off Rome to her, had longed for her to see where they lived, to approve Umberto's care of her mother...

Reviewing her behaviour since she'd arrived, seeing it through her mother's eyes, she felt wretched, ashamed—and the fact that none of it had been meant made absolutely no difference.

'I'm sorry,' she apologised miserably. 'I truly didn't mean to be rude to anyone; it's just that if I can't find anywhere for the animals they'll have to be put down—and that would break my heart.'

'As it's breaking mine to see you so—unlike yourself.'

It was a gentle reproof, emphasising that people were more important than animals, which, of course, was true. 'I'm sorry,' she said again. 'But—'

'No buts,' her mother rebuked her softly. 'Just try to see it from someone else's perspective. For the first time in his life Umberto has someone to show off, someone to shower affection on. They're very family-orientated, the Italians, and all his cousins, nephews, nieces, uncles—all have children, wives, people to parade, talk about—'

'And poor Umberto only has me.'

'Yes, and, oh, Rea, not once have you bothered to dress up, make up your face—'

'But I didn't bring anything!'

'I know—because you weren't intending to socialise,' she said sadly.

Eyes wide, staring at her mother's reproachful face, she gave a long sigh and wondered futilely why all life's problems had to come along at once—like buses. 'I'll make it up to him, I promise.'

'Not because you have to, Rea...' her mother began, and Rea felt doubly wretched—not only that her mother should think so, but because it might be partly true. She *did* love him, and should have realised the importance of her visit—*would* have understood it before all this business with the land had brewed up.

'No, not because I have to,' she promised. 'Because I want to; because I wouldn't willingly hurt him for the world. Or you. I'll even apologise to Tano,' she added, managing a faint smile. 'But I truly didn't know you rented the apartment from him.'

'We don't rent,' her mother denied. 'It's his.'

Shocked, Rea exclaimed, 'You mean he lives here? Permanently?'

'Yes. You must have known this was a different address to the one I gave you!'

'No—no, I didn't. I didn't look at the address when we arrived from the airport. Why should I have? And when you said about the telephone number being different I merely assumed you'd had it changed for some reason.' It was something else she hadn't paid attention to. Then she frowned. 'But I got a letter,' she began, confused.

'Of course you got a letter! Umberto picks the mail up from our apartment each morning!'

'Then, if you have an apartment of your own, why are you here?'

With a funny, appealing little smile, and a definite blush, her mother murmured, 'Because Umberto wanted me to have one of those baths that bubble—er—'

'A Jacuzzi?'

'Yes. *I* didn't want one, but there was one at the hotel where we stayed on our honeymoon and—'

'And you had a really great time huddling in it together?' Rea guessed, with a little choke of laughter.

'Yes—and just because I'm fifty doesn't mean I don't—'

'Enjoy sex?' Feeling more like crying than laughing, she hugged her mother tight. 'Oh, Mum,' she choked. Pulling herself together, she leaned back and managed a smile. 'Well, go on; Umberto wanted you to have a Jacuzzi, and...'

'And he tried to do the plumbing himself.'

Her laughter bubbling over, because she knew very well by her mother's expression that he'd insisted on doing it himself because he hadn't wanted to face any ribald comments a plumber might have made, she guessed, 'And cocked it up?'

Joining her daughter's laughter, she nodded. 'We flooded not only our apartment, but the one below.'

'And Tano invited you to stay here until yours was habitable again?'

'Yes. So you see, darling...'

'Why you were embarrassed. Yes, I do. I just wish someone had thought to explain it to me four days ago!'

'I thought I had. So you will apologise to him?'

'Yes,' she sighed. 'I'll apologise.'

'Nicely?' her mother prompted.

'Yes, Mother, nicely.' And it would be absolutely mortifying because—

'And he is looking for another piece of land for you, so your animals won't have to be put down, will they?'

'No,' she agreed shamefacedly. 'That was—'

'Emotional blackmail?'

'No. Peevishness.' Giving her mother a rueful smile, hope warring with guilt, she gave an infectious little chuckle.

'That's better,' her mother approved warmly. '*That* sounded more like you!'

'Oh, dear. Have I been that horrendous?'

'Uh-huh.'

'I'm sorry, but—'

'You're worried about your animals—I know. I *do* know, Rea, but it isn't Tano's fault, and he *is* going to a lot of trouble on your behalf.'

On her behalf, or because of Umberto and her mother? Which was why he had insisted she come, of course—not to discuss the land but because he thought she should visit her parents, which was absolutely none of his business.

'Now do come along,' her mother insisted briskly. 'Hurry up and have some breakfast; the coffee should still be hot. You don't want to miss the tour.'

No, she didn't want to miss the tour.

'Why don't you like him?' her mother asked as Rea hastily buttered a roll and spread it with jam.

'Tano? Oh, I don't know,' she murmured evasively. 'I just find him infuriating.' Infuriating? Oh, yes, really infuriating, and I keep having all these sexual fantasies about him—about wanting to tear his clothes off, leap into his bed, ravish him.

Oh, yes, she could really explain all that, couldn't she? Explain that the very first time she'd met him at her mother's engagement party it had been as though someone had hit her with a brick? She'd smiled—and he'd looked at her with amused contempt. And so she had told herself—convinced herself—that he was arrogant, full of self-importance, that he viewed life as a game. His game.

She'd known that he was wealthy and had assumed—again, wrongly—that he was some sort of playboy. She had since discovered, of course, that that wasn't true; he *did* have convictions—about archaeology. *Only* archaeology, it seemed.

Her mother had accused her of being selfish, but wasn't Tano guilty of much the same thing? She cared only about her animals—and he cared only about his artefacts. Yet she seemed to be the only one who thought so. Umberto liked and deferred to him. Her mother thought him charming. How could she think him charming? He didn't charm people, he ignored them. Most of the time anyway. Didn't even *see* them! Rome's answer to Indiana Jones.

And in insulting him she'd only insulted herself, she thought drearily, especially as it was his apartment she'd been insulting him in for the past week.

And it also infuriated her, she admitted honestly, the way women followed him—not only with their eyes! And he didn't even notice! Was quite oblivious! And now guilt and hormones—her stupid, stupid hormones that made a mockery of her mind's desire to dislike him—made her body yearn for a fulfilment she had never thought she wanted; it also made normal conversation with him impossible.

It hadn't only been her animals that had kept her from Rome, it had been Tano too, because she had known that she would have to meet him again, and had been afraid that her feelings wouldn't stay hidden. As they hadn't. Yet when she'd got his letter she'd rushed out like an adolescent, hope warring with common sense. Such a fool.

One eye on the clock, grateful that there was no time for her mother to probe further, Rea hastily swallowed her coffee and hurried off to shower and dress.

When she was ready, dressed in the jeans her mother so despised and a comfortable cream top, she quickly phoned Lucy to make sure everything was all right, begged her to try and find something else—*anything* else—kissed her mother, grabbed her bag, the guidebook Umberto had given her, and fled.

Not entirely sure, despite the map in the guidebook, where the Vatican was in relation to herself, she caught a cab, and, her mind rather more on her own concerns than the view, she continued to brood on that morning's argument.

Apologise, her mother had said. How could she apologise? The words were already sticking in her throat without even an attempt to utter them! Anyway, it hadn't entirely been her fault. Yes, it had. Had she really changed so much? Become so awful?

With a long sigh she snapped open her guidebook. The Vatican library, she read, 'holds world-famous manuscripts, including the first map of America after Columbus' discovery...' Would Tano one day be in a guidebook, named for some famous discovery? Or on the police list of famous murders because she'd whacked him over the head with a priceless antique? A Pict artefact maybe?

Which brought her back to her mother's accusations—justified accusations. She knew she was impatient, forceful, that she didn't take time to soothe people's feelings—not because she couldn't be bothered but because time seemed to be forever pressing onward, because there was always so much to do. She had never taken time to stop and stare, and now, perhaps, didn't know how to.

But how could she confess to her mother that most of her behaviour towards Gaetano was prompted by sexual awareness and guilt? She couldn't.

And then there was Lucy, who'd sounded evasive, she thought, with a frown. Trying to persuade herself that it had been her imagination when she knew it hadn't, she absently closed the guidebook and stared from the window.

'Via del Corso,' the cab driver said helpfully.

'What? Oh, *grazie*.' As she stared along the famous street, without any prompting her subconscious provided information—one of the smartest shopping areas in the world, one mile in length, where ancient Romans used to race their horses. Now, how had she known that? Had she picked it up by osmosis? Or had she actually listened when Umberto had been enthusing about his city?

With a faint smile, and whilst they were halted in the traffic, she momentarily tried to imagine how it had been. Full of noise, laughter, cheers? And had those ancient Romans bet on the outcome of the races? Had *they* got into trouble with their mothers for being too single-minded? Probably, she thought, with another despairing sigh. Especially if they had been anything like herself.

Glancing in the opposite direction, eyes unfocused, she only slowly became aware that she was staring at Tano. Craning round further, she watched him chatting to some other people on the steps of a building. A roll of paper was in his left hand, and he used it like a baton to emphasise some point he was making.

There was a woman beside him—tall, elegant, smartly dressed. A colleague. Or was it Desirée? Rea saw her smile at him, saw him smile lazily back—a nice smile, warm and charming. He never smiled at her like that. But then she never smiled at him.

Snapping her eyes away, thankful when they began to move, she stared fixedly at her guidebook. He'd looked—impressive, in control, and devastatingly attractive. Tano, whom she must apologise to. Nicely. Perhaps that was the answer—being nice to him. Perhaps then he'd let her have the land.

And pigs might fly, she thought despondently. And if he ever found out what she'd done he would naturally assume that her being nice was just another ploy.

Alighting outside the Vatican, she paid the driver, then joined the queue, but her mind remained on Tano, and even once inside it took a conscious effort to dismiss him, to concentrate on what she was seeing and hearing as the tour guide explained all that they passed. Afterwards she would probably not have been able to say what she had seen, before they'd reached the Circular Hall, where they stared at the huge statues of ancient gods and heroes. So much history. So *much*. And it spoke for itself; it did not need—energising.

Staring at beautiful sculptures that teased at the mind, allowed her to marvel at their perfection, at the skill of those ancient people in carving marble into wonder, she gave a sad sigh. She had no talent like this—a talent that deserved to be fought for; all she could do was care for sick and injured animals—and disappoint people who loved her.

Umberto and her mother were the only family she had, and she remembered suddenly something she had once read: Love was the only thing you had to earn. Everything else you could steal.

And she hadn't earned it, she realised, only taken it for granted. She sighed deeply, unaware that her tour party had gone on without her, and wandered round the hall until she came to the bust of Antinous—the one who looked like Tano. And he *did* look like him—certainly he had that same indifferent gaze as he stared at her. And it *hurt*, dammit! She wasn't as selfish as he thought—at least, she didn't think she was.

Moving on to Hadrian—Hadrian who had built the wall—she reached out a tentative finger, touched his cheek. 'What was he like?' she whispered. 'Your young friend Antinous? Difficult? Was *his* behaviour contradictory?' Hearing footsteps, she self-consciously removed her hand, moved quickly on, hurried to catch up with her own group.

Some three hours later, her mind a blur of tapestries that looked painted, and ceilings of unutterable splendour, she felt exhausted, and incredibly humble, and wretched—because she was cheating, because she had done something that quite honestly appalled her. The fact that it had been done in desperation was no excuse whatsoever. And blaming it all on Tano was even more despicable.

She would ring Lucy again when she got back, impress on her the urgency of finding something else. She hadn't even remembered to ask her about one of the foxes—their latest addition. It had been run over and she was very doubtful about being able to save it. She wasn't even sure that they should. It had been very badly mangled. And if it was never able to be returned to the wild...

Walking out into St Peter's Square, blinking in the bright sunlight, she stared up at the columns that paraded triumphantly on all sides. Two hundred and forty saints and popes, all crafted by Bernini. And in the centre, she thought, with a wry smile as she remembered her comments to herself the night before, was the Egyptian obelisk. And around her were the seven hills of imperial Rome, the Eternal City. So forget your animals for a little while, she told herself. Take the time to stop and stare.

And so, instead of taking another cab, she began to walk in the direction of the Colosseum. She stopped at a café in a pretty little square for lunch, and, as she had promised herself, sat and stared, and wished for the first time since arriving that she had bothered to learn the language.

An elderly English woman asked if she might join her, then plumped herself down with a sigh of relief.

'An overdose of culture?' Rea asked gently.

The woman grinned. 'Do you know, dear, I think I'm even more muddled than when I started? All those statues and things. All so—well, *old*. BC some of them. I mean, *think* of it! So clever they were, to chip and chisel at marble until it was somehow more human than the humans they represented. And so beautiful some of them. Such beautiful men.'

'Yes. I wonder if they really looked like that? And all with nice legs!'

'And curls!' her companion continued. 'Not one with straight hair!'

No. Did Tano have nice legs? she wondered, then gave a sad little smile. She could just imagine his reaction if she asked him. 'You're on a coach tour?' she asked.

'Yes. And escaping from my companions for just a few minutes because I'm in *dire* need of a coffee!' Thanking the waitress, she stirred in sugar, drank with the greatest sigh of pleasure that Rea had ever heard, then got reluctantly to her feet once more. 'Onward,' she cried. 'Ever onward.'

With a little chuckle, Rea watched her disappear into the crowds. Finishing her meal, and leaving a generous tip because the service had been excellent, she gathered up her belongings and began to make her slow way—onward, she thought, with another smile.

She gazed dutifully at the grandeur of the Roman Forum—once the political and commercial centre of the city, or so her guidebook said—at the arches of Titus and Constantine, and the Colosseum—symbol of the Eternal City and classified as one of the seven wonders of the world.

Relaxing for what felt like the first time in weeks, she leaned against a nearby wall and allowed the May sunshine to warm her face, continuing to stare round her. Rome was a truly beautiful city, filled with extraordinarily nice people.

Watching a nearby tour group—English—she was amused to discover that they had all adopted the Italian habit of arm-waving to emphasise a point. A few days ago they would probably have quietly conversed, and now they had become very Latin. It was so easy to become absorbed into the Italian way of life...

Startled, she suddenly realised that it would be easy if she allowed herself—if she had not been making a conscious effort *not* to be charmed. And why had she? Because of her ambivalent feelings toward Tano? Or because she didn't want to go back to a fight that had lost its meaning, to wrangle over a silly piece of land just because she'd been annoyed at Tano's high-handedness?

No, that couldn't be true. It was the only piece of land there was. And the reason it was so difficult to find anything else was because farmers—councils—didn't want wildlife shelters on their land. She had never quite understood why. Animals had rights too, didn't they? People went on about saving the environment, but animals *were* the environment.

You're supposed to be stopping and staring, she reminded herself ruefully. Focusing on the scenery, the people, on a way of life that is so different from your own. She fought the admission that she was deliberately denying the assiduous tug on her emotions by this lovely city. It was full of warmth and laughter, an ambience that was undermining all her resolutions. Was that why she was being so dismissive of everyone and everything? Because she was so afraid to—enjoy?

Feeling confused, and really rather lonely, she saw Gaetano climbing toward the gardens on the Palatine Hill. A man who knew where he was going. *He* didn't need to stop and stare. The roll of paper was still clasped in one hand, and his long, jean-clad legs easily negotiated the steep steps two at a time.

More than one person turned to stare after him. It was the first time she'd seen him in jeans—clean ones at that. They emphasised his taut thighs, fitted his backside... Feeling herself flush, she glanced quickly round to make sure no one had seen, and wished with all her heart that she could stop having these stupidly erotic thoughts.

'Why don't you like him?' her mother had asked, and she'd said that it was because he infuriated her—as he did—because he didn't see her as a person, because he always dismissed her as—irrelevant.

But that wasn't strictly true. She'd disliked him originally because he'd reminded her of Piers, a man she had once loved. Piers, who had hurt her very badly. Sophisticated, exciting, he'd brought his dog into the vet's where she'd been working as an assistant.

At eighteen she'd been bowled over by his charm, had hung on his every word. He'd shown her a world she hadn't known existed, taken her out and about to sophisticated places, made love to her. Her first lover. And then he'd got bored with her wide-eyed innocence, her gauche professions of love, and so he'd gone off with his fancy friends, left her bewildered and hurting.

Never again, she had vowed. Never again would any man be allowed to do that. And no man had, she realised. Long after the pain had faded, her vow had stayed strong; she'd continued to keep men at a distance. But not on a conscious level, she thought; just with an internal, protective barrier.

And now, years later, along had come Tano, the same type—seemingly the same type, she mentally qualified—generating the same feelings. The same alarming needs.

Consciously admitting something she'd been refusing to face, knowing that she'd been disparaging him in order to negate her feelings, she sighed. She was no longer eighteen, but the muddle was still there. That was the trouble with stopping and staring; it left you time to think, and thinking could turn—personal.

But she did have to apologise, and here was an opportunity to do so. Before she could change her mind, she hurried after him, and when she reached the top of the steps she saw him ahead of her. Running up behind him, she grabbed his arm. 'Tano, I—'

Without taking his eyes away from whatever he was staring at, he ordered unemotionally, 'Go away.'

'But I . . .'

Disengaging his arm, he walked on and into a clump of trees.

'Tano!' Hurrying after him, breaking into a run, she didn't see the hole opening up before her, and then it was too late.

CHAPTER THREE

HER arms windmilling madly, Rea's cry of alarm was cut off abruptly as a strong hand grabbed her arm and hauled her to safety.

'Of all the stupid places to leave a hole!' she gasped breathlessly. 'Someone could fall and break their neck!'

'Don't tempt me,' Tano said softly.

Snapping her head round, she opened her mouth, then closed it again. Taking a deep breath, she reproved him shakily, 'If you hadn't run off like that—'

'I never run,' he dismissed coldly.

'—then it wouldn't have happened!' she gritted. 'And how am I supposed to apologise when you won't even listen?'

'Apologise?' he asked in palpable astonishment.

'Yes. For shouting at you this morning. For, well, you know...' Her fright dissipating, and unfortunately sounding about as apologetic as a Christian about to be fed to a lion, she added aggrievedly, 'I didn't *know* it was your apartment! All right? Although, the way you're behaving, anyone would think you didn't even notice you were being insulted!'

His face still and expressionless, he said quietly, 'I noticed.'

Avoiding his eyes, belatedly remembering her vow to be nice, she muttered, 'Yes, well, I was in a temper.

I was hoping you'd spoken to Resnick and that it could all be resolved.'

'It is resolved,' he said flatly. Shoving his roll of paper into his back pocket, he moved to the other side of the hole.

But not the way I want it to be! she thought. Watching him as he began to unravel some fencing, she bit her lip. Obviously the hole *was* about to be fenced in. And he looked so disciplined, which made his outburst earlier all the more extraordinary. A moody expression on her face, she automatically grasped the upright he plonked in front of her.

'Make yourself useful for once,' he ordered mildly. 'And don't let go.'

Bracing herself as he picked up a mallet and began to hammer the posts in, she wondered if she ought just to confess what she had done. He'd be cross but maybe not *that* cross. Maybe he would even understand—only, she couldn't seem actually to get the words out, not to say them and make them sound reasonable. 'You're just being obstreperous,' she murmured. 'It can't make any earthly difference to you if I put some sheds on the land.'

Handing her the mallet to hold, he took some twine from his pocket and wired the two end-posts together, briefly tested the tension, retrieved the mallet, and would have walked off if she hadn't stopped him. Try being nice, she told herself. Just *try*, Rea. You'll never know if you don't try.

'Subsidence, is it?' she asked, with every appearance of interest as she peered into the hole. Very fortunately, she didn't see the look he gave her.

'We think it's a cellar,' he replied. 'Last night's rain finally weakened the covering—a covering we thought to be infill.'

'Oh.'

'You've finished playing tourist?'

'I wasn't playing,' she denied. Finally looking up at him, she forced herself to smile.

'Weren't you?'

'No. I was just about to look at the Colosseum when I saw you, and then I was going to the church of St Peter in Chains,' she explained, trying for bright interest.

'But not with any enthusiasm, I take it?'

'Of course with enthusiasm! I have a lot on my mind,' she excused more moderately.

'Haven't we all? You don't wish to inspect the spot where the she-wolf was supposed to have suckled Romulus and Remus?' he enquired smoothly, with a nod to where it had supposedly occurred.

Sarcasm? 'I'll look later,' she muttered awkwardly.

Surveying her for some moments in silence, he finally observed, 'It won't work, you know.'

'What won't?'

'You being nice to me.'

'I'm not being nice to you!' she denied crossly. 'Well, I mean, I am, but not because...'

'You want my land?'

'No! I was interested.'

'How interested?'

'What?' she asked blankly.

'Because if you *really* wish to learn about ancient Rome, *really* wish to impress Umberto—'

'I'm not trying to impress anybody!'

'Really want something worthwhile to do, you can give me a hand.'

'Doing what?' she asked suspiciously.

'Digging. I'm short of able bodies at the moment. The students won't be available until their summer break, and due to the antiquities department being short of funding I need all the help I can get.'

Unpaid, presumably. Not that she wanted to be paid. Not that she wanted to work for him; she had enough work of her own. 'Can't Umberto help? He works in the antiquities department, doesn't he?'

'Yes, but no, he can't; he's in charge of finance. He's a curator.'

'Oh.' She hadn't even known that, had she? Although he hadn't needed to sound so derisive. 'You want the cellar cleared?'

'No, this can wait. I need people in the tunnels. They're extending the Metropolitana—'

'I know,' she broke in defensively. 'I'm not a complete ignoramus. Umberto said something about it.'

He nodded, accepting or dismissive she didn't know; his expression didn't change. She wondered if it changed when he made love to his Desdemona, or whatever her name was. Only, she didn't want to think about him making love to his girlfriend; it made her feel sick, especially if she was the extraordinarily sophisticated-looking woman he'd smiled at earlier.

'And seemingly everywhere they dig,' Tano continued, 'they came across ruins, artefacts, valuable antiquities. They are getting just the tiniest bit fed up with trying to find a route that *doesn't* run through ancient foundations, storehouses, whatever, and so every time they come across something—or every time they *admit* to having come across something—I go down to view it, and give my expert opinion. At the moment I am the most hated man known to the Metro diggers.'

The most hated man for a lot of other people as well! she thought. Not *only* the Metro diggers. And every time he spoke her mind wandered into fantasy. The way his mouth moved, his hands—

'And soon, I fear, a decision will be made that the Metro is more important than the ruins they desecrate.'

Jerking her attention back, she offered quickly, 'I imagine it's difficult, anyway, with catacombs running everywhere.'

'Not under the city itself; the ancient Romans had a powerful taboo on burying their dead or even the ashes of their loved ones inside the city walls, but outside the catacombs stretch for around five hundred miles.'

'Do they?' she asked limply. 'I didn't know that.'

'No.' Nor much else, his tone seemed to imply. 'You've been down?'

'Yes. It was very interesting. But I'm afraid I shall have to decline your offer to help with the digging; if you won't rent me your land I shall have to go home—try to find something else.'

God, she thought despairingly, she sounded like some Victorian maiden who'd just received an immoral offer, and she was sick to death of being defensive and—ignorant.

He nodded. 'Let me know if you need a lift to the airport.'

'I shan't,' she denied. 'And you don't need to say it with such *hope*!' Enough was enough. Nice? He wouldn't know nice if it bit him. And yet, just for a moment, she'd thought that his lips had twitched. No, don't be stupid, Rea; it had probably been derision.

'You don't wish me to tell you about the Casa di Livia?' he asked softly.

Oh, God.

Taking a deep breath, she swung round and, a look of helpless entreaty in her eyes, exclaimed, 'Don't! Please don't! I *am* sorry! I don't *mean* to be like this! It's just...'

'Frustration?' he asked softly.

Alarmed then unsure, because frustration could mean—anything, she searched his face, then sighed. 'Tell me about the Casa di Livia. If you have time,' she tacked on.

'I have time.' He smiled, not *very* mockingly, and took her arm. 'It has some extraordinarily fine examples of interior decoration,' he murmured blandly as he led her across the grass. 'And the contrast between delicate fresco painting and the grandiose ruins all around couldn't be more striking.'

'It couldn't?'

'No.'

'Extraordinary.'

'Yes,' he agreed drily. 'And if Augustus and his empress did not actually live there then it was the sort of decor with which they were familiar.'

'Fascinating.'

'Mmm. A walk through Rome is a walk through time,' he added, even more softly. Squeezing her arm, sending the most delicious shiver through her—an *unwanted* shiver, she thought firmly—he angled toward the north-east corner.

'And here on the Palatino,' he continued, sounding as though he was thoroughly enjoying himself, 'has been, in turn, a prehistoric fortress, a chic residential area, and, after the Decline and Fall—you have heard of the Decline and Fall...?'

'Uh-huh.'

'Part of it became a pleasure garden of the Farnese family.'

'Which part would that be?' she asked with teasing innocence.

He glanced at her, nodded as though in approval, which was slightly confusing, and solemnly pointed.

'Ah.'

'And here,' he explained as he drew her to a halt, 'in the ruins of what was once the imperial box, you can see the Circus Maximus. Can't you?'

Staring at the dusty oval below them, she nodded.

'See the garlanded emperor as he presided over the chariot races?' he encouraged mesmerisingly. 'See the crowds, the splendour, the squalor? Hear the cheering?' Languidly waving one arm to encompass another area, he queried, 'Can you see the laundry? Feel the heat, the steam? And the busy markets? Can you visualise the clothing, Rea? The togas, the sandals, the contrasts of white and purple and gold? The grinding poverty and the magnificence?'

Turning her slightly, he murmured, so close to her ear that she felt his breath, felt the hairs on her neck prickle, 'And here is the step where Caesar died, here the baths built by Septimius Severus. Look *inward*, Rea.'

She tried, but, conscious of his nearness, his magnetism, she saw only him—the sharp profile, the short hair, the mouth that she wanted to touch with her own—and then someone called his name and the spell was broken. Fighting disappointment because his voice had been so warm, so hypnotic, she turned and saw a liveried chauffeur, one arm raised to draw Tano's attention.

'Ah, duty calls. Excuse me,' he murmured. Staring down at her, amused mockery in his eyes where she had expected to see enjoyment, he lightly tapped her cheek. 'A little word of advice, Rea. Don't chase a man who might not want to be chased.' And then he was gone, striding away across the ruins—and she felt as though she had been slapped. All the enjoyment, pleasure, was gone. He'd been laughing at her. And it—hurt.

Stiffly defensive, mortified, she followed more slowly, and, leaning on the wall at the top of the steps, watched him stride towards a black limousine. The chauffeur held the rear door open with the deference given to important people and Tano climbed into the back—beside the extraordinarily sophisticated woman who'd smiled at him so devastatingly earlier.

Rea wanted so badly to hate him—and couldn't, because he'd shown her what he could be like. And why had he done that? To prove he was capable of seduction? To make her understand why women followed him in droves? Which they did, according to her mother anyway. Rea hadn't actually seen evidence of it, only the way women smiled at him. Was that how he behaved with Desdemona?

Depressed, and then angry with herself for believing his gentle teasing, she continued to stare before her. And if the chauffeur hadn't come? How soon would he have become bored with his game? Or had he been expecting the chauffeur and just been filling in time? *Was* he important?

She wasn't really sure what the little flag on the front of the car had implied, but it had looked like the symbol of the Italian government. All a bit out of your league, Rea, she thought. But she had apologised. Hadn't she? And he'd seemed to accept it, had even smiled at her...

Unaware of the faint, wistful curve to her mouth, she continued to stare ahead of her. Perhaps he didn't totally dislike her. Oh, stop it, Rea; stop trying to persuade yourself of something you know to be untrue.

Heaving a sigh, wanting suddenly to be home, where important people from antiquities departments didn't ride around in chauffeur-driven limousines and didn't disturb her, she slowly descended the steps. Better get on with her tour—and as soon as she got back to the apartment she would ring Lucy, see if any progress had been made, emphasise that she must find *something* before Gaetano found out—before mockery shattered on the rocks of deceit and became fury.

'Tom will help,' she told Lucy when she'd returned, hoping it was true. 'And I'll get the first available flight back. No, don't worry, everything will be fine,' she encouraged, with more hope than conviction. 'Just do the best you can.'

Slowly replacing the receiver, still aware of something in Lucy's voice that she couldn't put her finger on, she then rang the airport.

'Monday?' she exclaimed worriedly. 'Nothing sooner? No, all right; book me on that... Yes, yes,

put me on standby as well . . . OK, thanks, I'll pick
the ticket up at the desk.'

Monday? That was a nuisance, but there was
nothing she could do about it, except hope that
someone didn't turn up for his seat over the weekend,
although the airline clerk hadn't said how *many* were
on standby.

As she was about to push her bedroom door open
the phone rang, and she hurried to pick it up. It was
Mike Resnick saying that the new photographs still
showed nothing.

'Ask him if he wants me to take any more, will
you?' he went on.

'Yes, of course—er—do you think that means there
isn't a settlement there?' she asked hopefully.

'No idea. Gaetano's the expert, and I've never
known him to be wrong.'

'Oh.' Hardly encouraging. 'OK, thanks for ringing.
Yes, yes, I'll tell him. Bye.'

Slowly replacing the receiver, for a moment—just
one little moment—she wondered if she could forget
to tell Tano just for a few days until she'd moved
everything off his land. A few days weren't going to
make any difference, were they? Because if she told
him, and then he rang Mike, mightn't Mike ask why
there were sheds on the land? Perhaps she should have
asked Mike not to mention them . . .

Horrified by the way her thoughts were heading,
she sighed. She'd have to tell him; her behaviour had
been bad enough without adding further deceit. And,
anyway, he might accept that if the new photographs
showed nothing it was because there was nothing to
see. And, if Tano was busy, with luck he wouldn't

contact Mike until next week ... It wasn't as if it was urgent or anything ...

'O, what a tangled web we weave, When first we practise to deceive!' she quoted to herself. Her mother would be horrified. *Umberto* would be horrified—and Tano would be furious if he ever found out. Too late now to wish that she hadn't been so stupid ... She had better tell him at once. It might even turn out for the best.

False hope, Rea, she berated herself. What would be best would be to go home, forget all about him. Yet had she forgotten him in the months following the wedding when she hadn't seen him? No. Had she managed to forget him this afternoon when she'd been looking at ancient monuments? Again, no.

Staring at herself in the mirror above the phone, she wondered what Tano saw when he looked at her. People told her that she was beautiful. She didn't know if that was true, and hated herself for wishing that Tano would think so.

Heaving a sigh, she walked along to the kitchen and pushed open the door. Her mother was busy at the stove, cooking the evening meal, and Umberto was 'helping'. The fact that his helping seemed to consist of stroking her mother's arm was obviously irrelevant. Pretending not to notice that, or the blush both gave, she asked casually, 'Either of you know where Gaetano is? I have a message for him. I saw him go off in some fancy limo earlier, but...'

With a movement that fooled nobody Umberto put some space between himself and her mother. 'Visiting dignitaries from Milan, interested in his restoration work,' he murmured as he picked up a knife and began chopping a carrot as though it were his sole role in life. 'And then I think he was going to the institute. He wanted to check something, I believe—a mark, a signature. He found something in one of the tunnels and wanted to look it up.'

'Oh. How long will he be, do you think?'

'Hard to say. If he does not find for what he is searching . . .'

'Oh.'

'Is a problem?'

'No, not really. Are you expecting him back for dinner?'

'No, he said he would probably be late. You know how he is when he has something on his mind. He will wish to solve the problem this evening.'

Thoughtfully chewing her lip again, feeling restless and uncertain, she stared at nothing.

'You wish for me to run you down?' Umberto asked kindly.

'Hmm? Oh, no, I can get a cab or something,' she murmured vaguely. Although, if she sought him out, would that be classed as chasing? Well, she wouldn't give him that satisfaction.

'Tut-tut, so wealthy, Rea?' he teased. 'Come, I will drive you.'

'No, don't be silly.'

'Is not silly. I do not like you out on your own in the evening. Is not always safe.'

'Neither is missing dinner!' her mother exclaimed tartly.

'We won't be long.' Umberto smiled. 'Come,' he encouraged Rea. 'We will go now and be back very soon. Your mama and I are out this evening to visit friends; you wish to come? No,' he answered himself, 'you do not wish to come. Next time, perhaps. Yes?'

'Oh, Umberto, I'm sorry. I don't mean to be... Next time, I promise.' Only, the next time she would probably be in England. But she would come out again. Of course she would. But not for some time—not until she'd got over these ridiculous feelings for Tano.

'I won't go to the institute,' she decided, 'and I would love to come out with you both. I can leave Tano a message.' *That* couldn't be called chasing.

'You won't need to,' her mother said quietly, giving her daughter a smile of approval. 'I just heard him come in.'

'Then that is more fortunate.' Umberto smiled as he returned to his carrot-chopping. 'All will now be well.'

Yes. All would now be well, Rea thought, with a sigh. Taking a deep breath, she pushed into the hall, and, her voice stiff, stated bluntly, 'Mike Resnick rang. Nothing on the photographs.'

He nodded, began to step past her, looked as though he didn't even *see* her. Certainly his air of preoccupation didn't lift. Would it have lifted if Desdemona had been giving him the message? Probably. Hurt by his indifference, hurt that she actually cared, she opened her mouth to deliver the rest of what Mike had said, then gave a frustrated sigh when her mother came out of the kitchen, carrying a bowl of salad, and interrupted her.

'Gaetano!' she exclaimed, as though he was her delight, and, cutting through the rest of what Rea had

been going to say, added, 'Just in time for dinner.
And Claudia rang. She'll be here at seven.'

Slanting him a glance, Rea saw the corners of his
mouth turn down. Was Claudia also chasing?
'Perhaps her snake died,' she murmured sourly.

'Perhaps,' he agreed noncommittally. 'Although I
wasn't aware that Loredana had given it to her.'

'Ah.' She nodded understandingly. 'Loredana being
Desirée and no longer in the running?'

'Hasn't been for some time. Excuse me, would you?
I need to shower and change. No dinner for me, Jean;
I'll eat out.' Without waiting for any comment, his
air of preoccupation returning, he walked along to his
bedroom.

'That was unnecessary, Rea,' her mother reproved
quietly. 'Did you apologise?'

'Yes, but I don't think he was listening.'

'Rea!'

'Well . . .' Unable to explain that her irritation
stemmed from depression, because whatever she might
be feeling there was no way she could persuade herself
that he was feeling the same, she made a supreme
effort to pull herself together. Glancing at Umberto,
who was hovering in the kitchen doorway, she burst
out, 'I don't know how you can work with him! Does
he really not drive you insane?'

He gave a slow smile, then a shout of laughter.

'Umberto! You old fraud! Everyone keeps telling
me it's my imagination, that I'm being difficult—and
it isn't me at all! Everyone finds him difficult, don't
they? Go on, admit it!'

'He's very clever.'

'I didn't say he wasn't! Just lacking in communication skills.'

'Only when he wants,' Umberto confessed, his eyes twinkling with amusement as he ushered her into the dining-room, behind her mother. 'Or is not listening, or preoccupied—'

'Or deliberately obstructive. And how Mother finds him charming, I just don't know!'

'Your mother finds everyone charming.'

'Except me,' she said, with another downswing into despondency. 'I am sorry I've been such a pain.'

'Is understandable,' he said kindly. 'And if I had not been so proud of my new stepdaughter, had not wanted to show Gaetano your animal shelter, your new piece of land—'

'And if he hadn't seen something that led him to think it might be the site of a Pict settlement . . .' Tablemats were shoved into her hands and she stared at them rather blankly.

'Rea! Lay the table, there's a good girl,' her mother ordered as she bustled back to the kitchen.

Nodding, Rea laid the mats in place, then collected cutlery from the sideboard. 'I have to go back,' she confessed quietly, then glanced rather worriedly at Umberto. He would be disappointed, she knew. 'I'm sorry, but if I don't find something . . .'

'I know,' he agreed sympathetically. 'Is not much time, is there?'

'No.' There wasn't any time at all!

'And if you hadn't insisted your mother sell the house, keep the proceeds . . .'

'I could have used the garden, yes. Oh, well, I dare say something will turn up,' she added, with more confidence than she felt. 'I ought to ring Tom; perhaps he'll have time to look for something, think of an alternative.' Not that she held out much hope.

There you go again, Rea, thinking you're the only one who can do anything! she chastised herself. Had she always been like that? She had no idea; she'd never been given much to self-analysis, only knew that it was her life and she needed the ordering of it. She didn't know where the need had come from, only that it was so. As a child, naturally, her mother had had the ordering—so when had the roles reversed themselves? she wondered. When had she become the manager?

Her mother had always insisted, from when Rea had been quite young, that Rea mustn't get into the habit of thinking she had to care for her. Just because she was a widow it didn't mean she was incapable. And she wasn't.

There had been an almighty row when Rea was eighteen because she'd flatly refused even to consider going to university. The grant would never have been enough to cover her expenses and there had been no way that she had been going to allow her mother to dip into her meagre savings. What she hadn't understood then was that her mother would always feel guilty about what she called 'missed opportunity', but Rea had never regretted it.

With her mother's encouragement she had left home when she'd been eighteen, found herself a life of her own, working in a veterinary practice, and had become passionately involved in animal welfare. And then she'd started up her own kennels to meet the expense of caring for sick wildlife.

She and her mother had always remained the greatest of friends. So when had Rea begun to feel responsible for her? After Piers? Had she been somehow afraid that her mother would be duped as she had been duped? She really couldn't remember. But was that when she had begun to feel responsible for *everything*? And why? It didn't seem very logical if it was just because of a soured love affair.

And then when her mother had met Umberto Rea had insisted that she sell the cottage and keep the proceeds for herself, despite the fact that her mother had yearned to give the cottage to her daughter. Why could she never accept things graciously? Why did she always have to be the giver, and always arrogantly assume that she knew best?

She didn't always know best; if she did, she wouldn't be in this mess. She'd have got a proper lease from Ralph Bressingham, covering not only the use of his land for an animal shelter but parking for her American-style camper-van that she lived in—and which now resided on Tano's land.

Wrapped up in her own thoughts, she took her place at the table, helped herself to cutlets and salad, idly listened to Umberto and her mother discuss their plans for the evening, then became aware of Gaetano leaning in the doorway.

As he fastened his watch to his wrist, his eyes on what he was doing, the same preoccupation softening his face, she studied him. His was a truly beautiful face, drawn by an artist—the brows even, not too thick, cheekbones high, arrogant almost, the nose straight, exactly right, and the mouth and chin well shaped.

It was a mouth that she kept imagining touching hers, and she silently groaned, fought down the ache of desire that was so extraordinary, so worrying, that made it so hard to drag her eyes away from him. The shape of his skull, so clearly defined by the short hair, with his small, flat ears, was classical. Everything was in proportion—the length of leg, arm, the width of his chest and shoulders—even his teeth were perfect.

His lashes lifted so suddenly that she gave a little start, blushed, then cursed herself, widening her eyes in denial of being embarrassed as she was caught staring. He had beautiful eyes that at the moment were crisp and clear, far-sighted—not vague, unfocused as was so often the case. Or mocking.

What goes on in your head? she wanted to ask. What thoughts mill around in that clever brain? He lifted one eyebrow in query, and she blurted stupidly, 'You look like a cat burglar.'

A faint smile twitched his mouth as he glanced down at the black trousers and shirt he'd changed into. 'Perhaps I am.' With a last tug at his watch-strap he straightened and walked across to them. Resting one hand on her mother's shoulder, he said easily, 'Don't wait up, will you? I shall probably be late.'

Jean smiled up at him as though he were a favourite son. 'All right. Be careful. Have a nice time.'

'I will,' he returned solemnly, but there was a glint of warm amusement in his eyes. Bending, he dropped a light kiss on her hair, nodded to Umberto, and let himself out.

He didn't nod to me, Rea thought, then shook herself for her folly. 'Where's he going?'

'I don't know, dear; it isn't my place to ask. Out with Claudia, presumably.'

Bully for Claudia, thought Rea, but there was a sick feeling inside her—a sourness. Was Claudia sophisticated? Beautiful? And then she remembered that she hadn't finished giving him Mike's message. Oh, hell, she really didn't need any more accusations levelled at her. Shoving herself quickly to her feet, she murmured, 'Forgot to tell him something.'

She caught him upon the landing and blurted, 'I forgot to mention that Mike said to ring him back if you wanted any more photographs.'

He halted, turned, and because the landing was only dimly lit she couldn't really see his expression, could only feel his stillness. 'Forgot?' he asked softly as he returned to stand in front of her, place his hands on her shoulders.

Stiffening, wanting to shrug away from his touch yet not wanting him to know how he could affect her, she said defiantly, 'Yes.'

'And that's it?'

'Yes.' Nervous, almost frightened by the way he was looking at her, and with that awful sexual tension cramping her muscles, she shifted her feet, tried to ease free, used aggression to cope with these ridiculous feelings. And yet, if he'd smiled... 'I have to get back to my meal.'

'Should never have left your meal,' he corrected. 'What game are we playing now, Rea?'

'No game! I merely forgot to give you the rest of Mike's message, and—'

'Chased after me to do so. Then this time let us not, by any means, waste the chasing.'

'I was not chasing! And I haven't the faintest idea what you're talking about!'

'Haven't you? Do you not consider that I might be curious to see if there is anything inside you worth the love that Umberto and your mother lavish on you?'

'What?' she gasped.

'And why so nervous? It's what you want—what you've wanted since we first met.'

'*What* is what I want?' she demanded.

'To be kissed. By me.'

'No!' she denied, her eyes wide with alarm. 'You think I want to be kissed in punishment for wrongs only you perceive to be real?'

'Then how *do* you want to be kissed?' he asked softly.

'I don't want to be kissed at all! And how dare you assume . . .? You think I find you attractive?'

'No,' he drawled, 'I think you find me a challenge.'

'Don't be ridiculous,' she dismissed, and wished with all her heart that she could sound less breathless. 'You really think I want to become involved with you? That just because I came out about the land, because it's your apartment—which I didn't know—because I was rude you think you can use me to fulfil your sexual fantasies? You think I want to be your mistress or something?'

'I didn't ask you to be my mistress,' he pointed out with the same quiet mockery. 'And most of my sexual fantasies have already been fulfilled. Probably around the age of twenty-two.'

Yes, she could imagine. 'Then what do you want?'

'I told you.'

'No, you didn't; you just said some stupidly in-comprehensible—and it's utterly absurd!' she stormed. 'And, for the last time, I am not chasing you! You're the one who insisted I come! *And* not about the land!' she added. 'So if anyone is mis-leading anyone it's you! You insisted I come out be-cause you thought it was your right to interfere!'

'Of course,' he agreed, soothingly derisive.

'You did! And you're the last man I would ever want to be involved with!' Liar, liar. 'You're...'

'Yes?' he asked silkily. 'I'm...?'

A heartbreaker? Taking a deep breath, more frightened than she would have believed possible without even really knowing why, she argued desper-ately, 'It doesn't matter what you are! And *you're* the one who seems to be playing games! Nasty, nice, nasty... So let's just leave it at that, shall we?'

'Because I'm...?' he prodded again, an expression of determined patience on his face. He looked as though he were prepared to wait there all night to get a satisfactory answer.

'Leave it!' she gritted.

'No. I would very much like to know what you per-ceive me to be.'

'Why? What possible difference can it make?' Rock-like, he moved not a muscle, just waited. 'Oh,' she cried in exasperation, 'you manipulate people! Use them, discard them—all with that damned Cheshire-cat smile on your face! You make up your mind about people, arrogantly assume you're right... You don't *like* me! So just stop it, Tano! Just stop! I'm not a toy!'

'No,' he agreed. 'And it's *Gae*tano.'

'All right!' she shouted. 'Gaetano! Go find someone else to play with! Like Claudia. Presumably she'll be here any minute now.'

'Mmm, and I do not wish to play with Claudia,' he mused. 'She might take me seriously.'

'And you think I won't?'

'I know very well you won't.'

'Oh, *do* you?' she sneered. 'And what would you do if I did?'

'Walk away?'

'Yes!' she agreed, satisfied at being proved right. He would—the way Piers had walked away. 'You manipulate people, don't you? Calculate and weigh the odds very, very carefully. And then you do exactly as you please, when you please and on whatever reasoning you base your calculations! Well, I don't want to play! I *never* wanted to play! And if this is some hare-brained scheme to—'

'My schemes are never hare-brained,' he denied in calculated amusement.

'To make me go away,' she completed in grinding fury, 'let me tell you that I'm going home on Monday!'

'Not till Monday?' he asked in soft tones of severe disappointment.

'No,' she gritted. As she swung away, he pulled her back with just the right amount of force to bring her up against him, as though it had been practised. Often.

'Let me go.'

'No. And trading insults won't get you what you want,' he derided softly.

'You won't give me what I want so it doesn't matter, does it?'

'Doesn't it?' With a twist of his mouth, which on anyone else might have passed for a smile, he kissed her. Hard. Not hard enough to hurt, just hard enough for her to know that she'd been thoroughly kissed—a punishment that didn't punish at all.

And it was everything and more than she had ever imagined it might be—warm, destructive, shattering—and he didn't even give her the satisfaction of breaking it first. *He* broke the kiss, languidly moved her away and stared down at her. And then he smiled.

'The face of an angel,' he said softly, 'and the mind of a steel trap.' And with perfect timing the outer door opened. Turning, he ran lightly down the stairs—to Claudia.

An angel? Closing her eyes, Rea felt a little shudder run through her. It had happened so quickly, ended so suddenly, almost before she'd had time to savour the shaming delight of a hard body, a practised mouth, warm skin—and now he would know he'd been right about her, wouldn't he?

So why had he smiled? He'd kissed her as though it was an experiment, something he'd been told would be enjoyable but was resisting all the same, and then he'd smiled. Why? And why say...?

Grasping the railing of the landing, wanting—no, *needing* to know what Claudia looked like, Rea peered cautiously over. She couldn't see her face, only dark glossy hair, expensively styled, an amber silk outfit with a dark brown throw-over wrap—and well-shaped arms as they lifted to encircle Tano's neck, and the way his head lowered toward hers...

Feeling sick, she quickly shut her eyes.

'Rea?' A voice from inside the apartment called.

With a little start she ducked back from the stairs, turned, and called quickly, 'Coming.' Hurrying inside, she closed the door. Had he seen her? Heard her mother call? Well, she didn't care if he had, she thought defiantly. Examining her flushed face in the hall mirror to make sure that she didn't look—kissed, she buried her emotions as best she could, smoothed her hair, took a deep breath, and went to finish her meal.

It was gone two when he came in, and she had to admit that he was quiet about it—no stumbling around waking everyone up—and hated herself for this need to analyse, for her feelings that wouldn't obey her mind. She didn't *want* to feel like this, and didn't understand why she did. Surely, surely his mockery should have cured her of any lingering desire? It was a desire that she found quite inexplicable. She didn't *like* him!

You liked him earlier, a hateful voice whispered. No! He had never been the sort of man she might have chosen for herself. And it made her so *angry*! Her mind betrayed by her body. She had stood on that landing shivering like a frightened virgin, and he had *known*—that was what was so mortifying! He'd *always* known! And she could almost still feel his mouth pressed to hers, the strength of his fingers digging into her arms...

Did he now walk past her door with a derisive smile on his face? Did amusement still quirk his mouth? And it *had* been amusement—it had to have been.

But why? Because kissing her had been—funny? She wanted to get out of bed, pad along to his room, ask...

With a savage movement she flung herself over and determinedly shut her eyes. Enough! But at least she had pleased her mother and Umberto, she thought—gone out with them for the evening, met their friends. And that pleases you, does it? she asked herself almost despairingly. That you made someone happy? Didn't you even *enjoy* it? Didn't you do it because you *wanted* to? Yes, of course you did, and you *did* enjoy it; you just had so much else on your mind. You couldn't concentrate on anything else. Liar, she scolded herself. Liar. All you could concentrate on was his kiss, and the despair and desire it made you feel.

In the morning, more to distract herself than from any real desire, Rea went shopping with her mother, and when it began raining—when her mother went into the hairdressers—she reluctantly returned to the apartment.

Mooching around, disgusted with herself, furious with herself, and for want of something better, she began reading one of Umberto's archaeological books—very little of which she understood—and then in the late afternoon she thankfully abandoned it when Umberto came in, scattering raindrops.

'Hello, darling; is Gaetano here?'

'No, I haven't seen him.'

'Oh. I found what he was searching for.' Looking indecisive for a moment, he cursed softly under his breath, then grimaced an apology. 'He's probably at the site,' he grumbled quietly to himself, 'and I don't have time now . . . I have to see these people from the Milan institute . . . Are you doing anything important? Would you be an angel . . . ?'

Angel?

'No, I'm not doing anything.' What else could she say? She'd refused almost everything else the poor man had asked of her. 'You want me to find him? Give him a message?'

'Would you? I can drop you off . . .'

'Yes, of course. Give me a minute to get my shoes and mac . . .' And perhaps it would be for the best—to see Tano's expression in the cold light of day. *That* would cure her, wouldn't it?

Hurrying to her bedroom, she pushed her feet into flat leather shoes, grabbed her raincoat and accompanied Umberto down to his car. She could give Tano the note, ask casually why he'd smiled . . . And then what? she asked herself derisively. She was behaving like a schoolgirl, and that was shaming. Perhaps women never lost these fantasies. Perhaps when she was sixty she'd be lusting after some arthritic old colonel.

With a little grunt of laughter she stared out at the rain-washed city as Umberto fought his way skilfully through the heavy traffic, then out onto the Appian Way. Jolting over cobbles, not even very curious about where Gaetano was, she stared at dripping hedges, fleetingly glimpsed villas, and as the car slowed realised with surprise that they were near San Sebastiano.

'He's here,' Umberto exclaimed in relief as he pulled up behind Gaetano's battered red Citroën. Peering along the track to their left, he pointed. 'Is along there. You will get very wet,' he exclaimed worriedly as he glanced again at his watch. 'I cannot take the car any closer.'

'It doesn't matter.' She smiled. 'Just tell me where to go.'

Pointing along the track, Umberto explained, 'You will come to—er—boards surrounding a hole, and a hut for meetings . . .'

'Site hut,' Rea acknowledged. 'I'll find it. And the message?'

'Oh.' Scrabbling in his pocket, he produced a piece of paper. 'Just give him this.' Worriedly searching her face, he added urgently, 'Would it be a very great imposition to ask if you would get a lift back with Gaetano? I am going to be so very late . . .'

'No, you go; go on, and if Gaetano's not ready I can always get a bus or a cab or something.' Pressing a swift kiss to his cheek, she scrambled out, pulled up her raincoat hood, waved him away and began trudging up the narrow track.

As she rounded the bend she saw the site hut and, beside it, a hastily constructed sign which she couldn't read. Three heavy metal covers lay across what was obviously a trench, and the one nearest to her had been pushed back to accommodate a ladder. Leading to what—one of the Metro tunnels under construction?

Rapping on the hut door, holding her raincoat tightly round her neck to exclude the slanting rain which was coming down heavier than ever, she tutted, then tried the door and found it locked. Trundling round the side, she peered in the grimy window. Empty. Now what?

Eyeing the ladder, wondering if Tano could be down in the trench, she walked across and peered down. It wasn't dark exactly; there was obviously lighting of some sort, because she could see the faint glow, but she wasn't sure if she fancied climbing down the ladder, even though it was a short one.

'Gaetano?' she called tentatively, then listened. Unfortunately all she could hear was the patter of rain on the metal covers, the incessant drip from the surrounding trees, the faint sound of a car swishing past on the road behind her. Don't dither, Rea, she told herself; either go down or leave the message tucked in the hut door. And if it blew away, got wet, became indecipherable? That would be something else to level at her head.

With a sigh, and somewhat curious to see the conditions Gaetano worked in, she admitted honestly, she carefully swung herself down the ladder. Making very sure that her feet didn't slip on the wet rungs, she peered ahead. There was enough light from the pushed-back cover to illuminate the tunnel, enough light to see that it was a very *short* tunnel. Puzzled, she called softly, 'Gaetano?'

Nothing, and, curiosity being one of her besetting sins, and thinking that she would just have a *little* look, see what had brought Gaetano here, she carefully trod along the muddy boards, then gave a grunt of surprise. There was a doorway. Marble-edged, of all things!

Peering inside, she gave another blink of astonishment. Catacombs. Obviously already discovered catacombs because they were lit. Obviously, again, part of San Sebastiano. So why was there a doorway to nowhere?

Staring back the way she had come, expecting to see signs of something—artefacts, broken pottery, urns—she shook her head in bemusement when she saw nothing of the kind. So why was there a trench? Why was Gaetano down here—if he *was* down here? And if he was and had wandered into the tunnels she certainly had no intention of going in there on her own in order to look for him. With her luck she'd go the wrong way and end up wandering through all five hundred miles of them.

There was no harm in just looking, though, was there? At least then she'd be able to sound vaguely intelligent on the subject when he asked—*if* he asked.

Ducking her head, carefully negotiating the uneven floor, not intending to go out of sight of the doorway, she stared round her. Five hundred *miles*, she repeated to herself wonderingly. Trundling along with your dear departed loved one, excavating by lamplight . . .

And there were some very odd sounds down here, she decided nervously. Glancing rather apprehensively upwards, she assured herself that the faint rumbling she could hear was merely the sound of traffic on the road above.

'Tano?' she called, tentatively, hopefully. 'Tano?' Gaetano, she corrected to herself; he doesn't like to be called Tano. Tough. 'Tano?'

Glancing behind her, seeing that she was getting dangerously far from the trench, she halted, decided to go back. Perhaps even now he'd be at the hut, would want to know what on earth she thought she'd been doing. With a little grimace, convinced that she was right, she saw the light ahead of her change, diminish, and she frowned.

More clouds, that's all, she tried to tell herself. Thunder clouds, maybe, obscuring the light. But she hurried all the same—and discovered that some idiot had removed the ladder and pulled the cover over the end of the trench.

'Hey!' she yelled urgently. Breaking into a run, slipping and sliding on the wet duckboards, she grabbed up a handful of dirt, hurled it at the cover. 'Hey! Don't shut me in! Tano!'

Searching frantically round for something to use as a lever, something to knock with, she thought she heard voices from behind her. Whirling round, she called urgently, 'Tano?' Hearing no reply, and suddenly terrified of being left, she ran back, scrambled through the doorway into the catacombs, caught her foot on something, fell and knocked herself out.

CHAPTER FOUR

REA woke to silence and complete absence of light. Confused, bewildered, unable for the moment to remember where she was, she became aware of cold stone beneath her hip, grit under her outflung hand. 'Oh, no,' she whispered. 'Oh, dear God, no.' Now, don't panic, Rea, just don't panic, she told herself. You know where you are; you can get out. Of course you can get out.

But she didn't want to move, she found. She really didn't want to move—just wanted to close her eyes and make it all go away. But she couldn't do that because—because she didn't know how long she'd been down here, and if the lights were out that meant that—everyone had left.

Scrambling to her knees, she listened with every part of her being, tried to probe the darkness. And it was Friday, wasn't it? The start of the weekend...

'Tano?' she screamed.

''Ano, 'ano, 'ano,' came back faintly. Oh, God. And she was cold, she found, with that bone-chilling cold that came from fear.

Carefully moving into a sitting position, waiting hopefully for her eyes to accustom themselves to the dark—which they didn't—she called pathetically, 'Hello?' Her voice echoed back again eerily.

Oh, this was silly. *Someone* must know that she was down here. Umberto knew... Yes, but Umberto was at the institute, wasn't he? And what had obviously happened was that Tano had gone out through the catacombs, not knowing that she was looking for him, and the officials had closed and locked up before anyone had realised she was there.

But Tano would probably go to the institute, wouldn't he? He would speak with Umberto, and even now a very worried and anxious stepfather would be trying to find someone to unlock the site and let her out—if he'd finished his meeting, that was. If Tano had found him, that was.

And supposing he hadn't? Supposing Umberto's meeting went on for hours? Well into the evening? Well, you can cope with that, Rea, she told herself. A couple of hours... You've probably been here that long already... Oh, for goodness' sake! You only knocked yourself out! You haven't been in a *coma*!

Raising one hand, she carefully touched her fingers to her temple. Not even sticky—just a little bump and a bit of a headache. So, the thing to do, Rea, is to wait where you are, not to go stumbling around all these passages getting yourself thoroughly lost in the process—like those two tourists had last year, she suddenly remembered. They'd been missing for two days. You won't be missing for two days, Rea; don't be stupid.

Even if for some extraordinary reason Umberto didn't finish his meeting till midnight he would worry when she didn't arrive home. Her mother would worry. But supposing they went to bed, fell asleep, didn't find out till the morning...

Clamping down on hysteria, she tried to stay calm, and, with no way of calculating the time because she couldn't see her watch, it seemed like hours that she sat there. And there were noises, she discovered—little shushing noises, like whispers, and she felt goose bumps rise on her skin. Was that a footstep? Breathing?

'Tano?' she screamed, and her voice echoed and echoed along empty passages, frightening her more. 'Tano?' she whispered. 'Oh, Tano, please find me.'

And she couldn't sit here any longer—really she couldn't. If this was part of San Sebastiano—which it must be—then the church was only just around the corner, wasn't it? And perhaps she could find the exit into the church. *That* wasn't shut for the weekend, and perhaps if she was very careful, didn't panic, get confused, she'd be able to get up there, and someone would hear her, wouldn't they?

Or should she go back to the trench? Yes, she decided, the trench would probably be better.

Reaching behind her to lever herself to her feet, trying to keep the wall at her back at all times, her arm disappeared into a hole—a hole where a body had probably once lain—and she whimpered with shock.

Stop it! Now just stop it! she ordered herself.

Scrambling to her feet, she leaned back. Now, think, girl, think. You ran in a straight line before you tripped, and you rolled over and sat up, so in order to find the trench again you have to go left.

She went left for what seemed a very long way—much too long a way—got frightened, turned and went back. Beginning to feel really panicky, she took deep breaths to calm herself. Try again, Rea. No. You'll get lost. No, I won't. It's best to stay put. They always say stay put when people get lost.

Closing her eyes, which for some silly reason made her feel more secure, she tried to remember the layout when she'd first seen the catacomb four days ago, tried to remember if it had looked anything like it had looked before she'd fallen.

Had it seemed familiar? Had there been a fish symbol? An old lamp that hung before it, left by some ancient Roman, perhaps, or tomb robber... Shut up, concentrate. Had she seen anything like that? She didn't think so. But if she could find the fish, or the lamp, which would be easier to locate, then she would probably be able to find her way out to the church.

The lamp wasn't easier to locate. The lamp was impossible to locate, probably because she was in the wrong place. And a long time later, hopelessly lost, her face streaked with frightened tears of frustration, Rea sank back to the floor and cried.

She had always thought herself capable, competent and strong, and now, at the age of twenty-nine, she discovered that she was afraid of the dark, afraid of the ghosts that roamed this place, and beginning to feel desperately claustrophobic.

She was also terribly aware of the endless dark tunnels stretching away from her in all directions. Anything could be in those tunnels—rabid dogs, rats... Eyes wide, she stared at a tiny point of light... then screamed.

'Who's there?' a disembodied voice demanded.

Totally astonished, she whispered, 'Tano?' Belatedly realising that the pinpoint of light had been bobbing like a torch, she gave a choked little cry of relief. 'Here! I'm here!' she shouted stupidly. 'It's Rea! Oh, Tano, I'm here.'

'Where?' He sounded exasperated.

'Here! I can see the torch!' As the light grew brighter, drew nearer, throwing eerie shadows across the walls, she found herself staring at a carved piece of rock and she frowned—she didn't remember seeing that before—and then realised that the light had gone.

'Tano? *Tano!*' she screamed, and heard her voice echo round the empty passages, heard the faint echo in answer. 'Tano!' she yelled urgently. 'You've gone the wrong way!'

'Near...near...near...' the ghostly echo came back.

Was he asking what she was near? 'Carving,' she yelled. Oh, don't be bloody stupid Rea, she thought; there are hundreds of carvings in the catacombs.

Feeling frantically round her for something readily identifiable, she found there was nothing—nothing to pinpoint where she was. And there were so *many* intersecting passages that he could be stumbling around for hours without finding her!

'Calling...ing...ing,' echoed even more faintly.

Keep calling; yes, that was sensible. Shouting until she was nearly hoarse, she slowly registered the fact that his voice was louder, not so echoey. 'Here,' she repeated tiredly. 'Here, here, here...' And suddenly there he was. 'Oh, Tano.' Stumbling, she hurled herself into his arms, hugged him tight, dug her fingers into his back. 'I'm here.'

'So I see,' he observed drily as he automatically held her against his comforting length. 'But *why* are you here?'

'To find you, of course. I wasn't chasing you,' she added stupidly. 'And then I fell and knocked myself out. I thought I'd be here for ever, and oh, Tano, all the lights went out...' Feeling frantic, terrified that she was going to lose the only bit of human warmth she'd felt in what seemed like years, she clutched him tighter. 'Don't let me go.'

'No, I won't let you go. But *why* did you want to find me?'

'I had a message...'

'A message?'

'From Umberto, and then someone put the cover over the trench and I couldn't get out... Oh, Tano,' she gasped, with a last shuddering sigh. Raising her head, she stared at him in the light from the torch and found that she wanted to kiss him, press her mouth to his, never let him go. And maybe she did or maybe he did—she didn't really know who instigated it, only knew that his mouth was on hers, urgently, warmly, so desperately needed. And she flung her arms round his neck, held him impossibly tight, kissed him back with so much passion, so much need, and held him tighter and tighter and tighter.

Her heart beating erratically, her breathing agitated, she pressed kisses to his mouth, his nose, his chin, cheekbone—anywhere she could reach—registered the warmth of his palms against her back, the way his own mouth grazed across her face, sought and captured her mouth again and again until the pain inside her became excitement, desire, an erotic ache, and, without thinking, without plan, Rea stood on tiptoe, fitted her body to his, felt his warmth, his strength, his own desire—and that, just for a moment, gave her pause and shocked her back to awareness.

Leaning only her upper body away, she stared at him, searched his eyes—and suddenly realised what she had done.

'Sorry,' she muttered, embarrassed. 'I'm sorry.' Looking away, anywhere but at him, she added awkwardly, 'Relief—so relieved to see someone,' she explained jerkily.

'And anyone would have done as well?' he asked carefully.

'What? Yes,' she insisted in relief. 'Yes, anyone! Take me out of here,' she pleaded thickly. 'Please.' Mortified by what he must think, shutting her mind to the fact that he'd responded—or even instigated it—she took a deep, steadying breath. When he didn't reply she jerked her head back to look at him. 'You do *know* how to get out?'

'Yes, I know,' he agreed quietly.

'Good,' she babbled. 'But if the lights are out—'

'It means that someone has locked up and gone home.'

'Yes. But they must know *you're* still here!'

'Why must they?'

'Because your car's here!'

'But not outside the church. Riccardo put the cover back, you say?'

'Well, someone did; I don't know if it was Riccardo.'

'Then let's go and have a look.' Playing the torch over the walls and roof to get his bearings, he caught her arm and warned, 'Watch where you put your feet.'

He sounded all distant again. Why? Because she was being a nuisance? Because he was embarrassed at the way she'd flung herself at him? And why had she? She never behaved like that—as though she couldn't *cope*, as though she were some foolish little female that always needed a man around.

Dragging in a deep breath, trying desperately to regain control of a body that had gone to pieces, and needing desperately to fill the silence, she probed, 'I expect you know these tunnels very well.'

'Mmm, although I hadn't been in this particular one for years—not until the marble slab was found and we broke through here. The lights don't extend much further than you were. But why on earth did you move so far from the trench? If I hadn't been exploring some old tunnelling...'

'I didn't *mean* to! I—panicked,' she added shamefacedly. 'I kept hearing noises.'

And much to her surprise he didn't scoff, didn't denigrate her feelings, just halted, put a comforting arm round her shoulder and hugged her briefly to his side. 'Yes. Easy to imagine all sorts of horrors down here, isn't it? The first time I came I *knew* a wolf was following me. I could hear it breathing, almost see its eyes, its saliva dripping from long, long, fangs...'

'Did you?' she asked wistfully.

'Yes.' He didn't think it necessary to tell her that he'd only been ten at the time. With another smile, another hug, he urged her forward, then shone his torch across the marble arch, unaware how much he had astonished her. Moving into the trench, he played the beam over the metal covers. 'Fool,' he muttered to himself.

'You or Riccardo?'

'Riccardo.'

'Because you're never a fool?' she asked quietly.

He gave her an odd glance. 'Oh, yes, sometimes I can be as foolish as everyone else.' Carefully examining the cover, he finally pronounced, 'Well, I won't be able to shift that. Come on, let's try the exit to the church.'

It felt like a long time but probably wasn't before they finally reached the steps leading up to the church, but, despite their hammering on the door and making enough noise to wake the dead, no one answered and hurried to let them out.

She had somehow expected that Tano would be annoyed or impatient, but he wasn't; he merely gave her a wry glance and tugged her to sit beside him on the top step. And switched off the torch. He obviously heard her gasp of dismay because he explained quickly, 'To conserve the batteries.'

'Oh.'

'Umberto knows you're here?'

'Yes,' she admitted quietly. '*He* asked me to come.'

'Hmm.'

'What does that mean?' she demanded suspiciously. 'He *did*. Even drove me here.'

He smiled. 'I don't doubt you.'

'Yes, you do! You think I'm chasing!'

His smile widened. 'Poor Rea.'

'Don't patronise me!'

He chuckled—a warm, intimate, sound. 'He was returning to the institute?'

'Yes,' she admitted stiffly.

'Then we have no choice but to wait.'

'No.'

'Cheer up; it could be worse.'

'How?'

'You could be on your own.'

'Yes.' With a little shudder, knowing how awful that would have been, how awful it *had* been, and then remembering her passionate greeting, she looked miserably down.

Hugging her arms round her knees, feeling awkward and constrained, she tried to tell herself again that her reaction had been caused by relief, a release from tension, and knew that it was only partly true. And he would be thinking that she had done it on purpose—because she found him 'a challenge'. And if she tried to justify her actions any further it would only give them an importance she didn't want them to have.

'You're shivering,' he commented softly.

'I'm all right,' she said quickly. She didn't want him to think that she wanted his arm round her again or something, even if he wanted to put it there, which he probably didn't. However, he did, and hugged her warmly to his side, rubbing briskly at her arm. And it was nice, a comfort because she was cold. And here in the near dark she felt little and lost, not like herself at all.

'Not as tough as you pretend, Rea?' he asked gently.

'No—does that make it easier to understand why Umberto and Mother love me?' she asked in a small voice.

'I've always understood why they love you. I only said those things because I was angry with myself, with you. Things said in anger should be forgotten.'

'Should they? Even if they have a basis in truth?'

'Yes.'

'Why were you angry with yourself?' she asked cautiously.

'It's not important.'

'And Claudia? Is she important?' Shut up, Rea; shut up. 'I mean,' she babbled on, 'because you looked a bit cross when Mum said she was coming.'

'Did I?' he asked noncommittally, then firmly changed the subject. 'Tell me why you consider all the sites proposed for your shelter too far away. Surely it doesn't matter where they are?'

With a little sigh, and, she supposed, grateful for something—anything—to take her mind off the warmth of him against her, to relieve the tension—*her* tension—she explained stiffly, 'Not if it was only for the wild animals, no. But it isn't, is it?'

'No. Too far from your tame vet?'

'No. And he isn't tame,' she protested.

'Isn't he? So why *are* the sites too far?'

Pushing her hands through her untidy hair in a gesture of weariness, then leaving them to rest on her aching temples, she explained, 'Because of the kennels—the kennels I need to run for the revenue they bring in to finance the wild animal shelter. Mostly I rely on regulars—who are in that area. I move areas and I lose the clients.'

'Not necessarily.'

'No, but probably. People don't want to travel long distances in order to leave their pets. They want to just pop down the road somewhere near—convenient. They don't want a long journey when they're probably already going on a long journey on holiday or something.'

'And there are other equally good kennels in the area?'

'Yes. And the first alternative site you proposed was almost next door to someone else's kennels,' she said in disgust.

'Oh. And the second?'

'Was in the middle of nowhere!'

'Ah. But if you didn't *need* the kennels...?'

'If I didn't need the kennels it would be different. But I do.'

'Or some other form of revenue to fund the shelter?'

'Yes. Only I don't have another source of revenue, do I? And that—' Breaking off, she stiffened and gave a primeval shiver. 'What was that?' she whispered. 'Did you hear it—a sort of sliding noise?'

'It's nothing,' he soothed. 'Truly. Traffic on the road above—'

'Traffic doesn't slide,' she pointed out, refusing to feel comforted.

'Then it's earth movement—settlement. Truly, Rea, it's nothing to worry about. Go on with what you were saying. "And that..."?'

'How can you remember what I said?' she burst out. 'How can you be so *calm*!'

'Because it's familiar,' he said gently. 'Nothing will happen to you, I promise. Go on.'

Her breath shuddery as she exhaled, feeling stupid and inadequate, she tried to remember what she'd been about to say. Mentally reviewing their conversation, she suddenly remembered. 'Oh, yes, and that idiot you sent along didn't have any understanding of the problems at all!'

'Idiot?' he queried softly. '"That idiot", as you call him, is a qualified environmentalist.'

'But he didn't know anything about my *needs*! Oh, Tano, I'm sorry; I really don't mean to be difficult but I don't know what to *do*!'

'And you aren't used to not knowing what to do, are you?'

'No,' she mumbled. 'I don't mean to be arrogant, impatient, but... I thought you'd invited me out to discuss it, but you hadn't, had you? You insisted I come out because you thought I'd been neglecting Mum and Umberto.'

'And hadn't you?'

'Yes,' she agreed, grudgingly honest, 'but not on purpose! I've been worried sick about everything. And now, if Bressingham is going to sue...'

'Don't worry about Bressingham. He won't sue.'

'How do *you* know?'

'Because I got my lawyer to write to him.'

'What?' Snapping her head round, forgetting for the moment that he was so close, her nose grazed his chin and she stiffened, drew back. 'You did? But why?' she managed.

'Because I thought you could use some help.'

'After everything I said?'

'*Because* of everything you said.'

'What does that mean?'

His smile was faint, barely seen. 'Home truths work both ways, Rea. My behaviour hasn't been faultless, and, like you, if something affects my work I'm often impatient, unseeing. Despite what you might think,

I *do* feel some responsibility for depriving you of your land.'

'Then couldn't I just use it for a little while?' she pleaded. 'A few weeks? Just until you're ready to dig?'

'But then you'd still have the same problems to sort out at a later date, wouldn't you?' he asked gently.

'But I wouldn't have them *now*. The badger's almost ready to be released into the wild, and one of the foxes—and the RSPB would maybe take the birds, and maybe Lucy could have the hedgehog and rabbit in her garden... If I just had some *time*!'

'You have a few weeks. Bressingham won't put you out into the lane.'

'Yes, he will,' she muttered morosely. Already has, she wanted to tell him, but if she told him now all this kindness and understanding would disappear, and she didn't want it to. Not now. Not here.

'Do the kennels fund it all sufficiently?' he asked curiously.'

'No,' she admitted despondently. 'I have a massive bank loan and only just about manage to pay off the interest. I was intending to extend, you see, before Ralph died—start up a cattery, be more *efficient*.' With a hollow laugh she began to pick at a piece of mud on her raincoat. 'Really efficient, huh?'

'Blaming yourself, Rea?'

'What?'

He gave an odd smile that she only barely saw in the gloom. 'Ever since I first met you you've been blaming everyone *but* yourself,' he pointed out gently.

'No! No,' she sighed. 'Not really. Only, because I was angry with myself for not being efficient—'

'You just lashed out?'

'Yes. These last few weeks have been a nightmare,' she confessed quietly. 'Frustrating and irritating. And now Lucy is being off and I don't know *why*.'

'Not having met Lucy, I can't say, but I am sorry about the land.'

'Sorry?'

'Yes. I wasn't being entirely arbitrary, you know; yet even if I'd kept my thoughts to myself it would have been discovered by someone else. We already knew about the ice well—'

'Ice well?' she queried in confusion.

'Mmm, we knew there was a Pict settlement in the area ... You did know that was how Umberto met your mother?'

'Because of an *ice* well?' she asked in astonishment.

'In a way. He'd been meeting with his counterpart at the British Museum; a local historian happened to be there—local to your mother, that is—and he asked Umberto to come down and look at the site of what they believed to be an ice well, and there he met Jean—'

'Who worked in the library where they held their historical society meetings,' she completed for him. 'But I didn't know about the ice well—something else I wasn't listening to,' she murmured defeatedly.

'Yes. And if *I* hadn't spotted the tell-tale signs someone else would have done. And I'd have been as furious as you are now if someone had wanted to use a piece of land I'd discovered to hold ancient artefacts in order to build a supermarket or an office block. Which is why I'm going to so much trouble to find you an alternative, because I *do* understand how you feel.

'And I can understand your dislike of me *now*, but not when we first met. Why did you dislike me so much, Rea?' he asked casually.

'What?' Suddenly wary, she gave him a nervous glance. Talking easily about her work was one thing, talking about her feelings was entirely another. 'You disliked *me*,' she said stupidly.

'I didn't know you; how could I dislike you?'

'You looked down your nose at me.'

Tano gave a grunt of laughter.

'Yes, you did! And I thought you were a playboy.'

'I don't have time to be a playboy.'

'Well, I didn't know that, did I?'

'And why dislike playboys so much?' he asked softly.

'I don't!'

'Don't you?'

Snapping her head round, picking up something he wasn't saying, she glared at him. If her mother had been talking... Not that her mother had ever met Piers, because at first he had been too new, too exciting to share, and then it had been too late. Anyway, Piers hadn't been a playboy, but had seemed just like Tano—wealthy and confident, devastatingly attractive. Although she couldn't really believe that her antipathy towards Tano stemmed from that youthful folly, how else was she to explain her feelings? Picking even more agitatedly at the mud, she jumped when he put his free hand over hers, then stiffened defensively.

'Just because we kissed it doesn't give me the right to probe?' he asked gently.

'No, and, anyway, I kissed you,' she muttered defensively.

'As a release from tension—yes, you said. And anyone else would have done just as well. Then why does my touch bother you?'

'It doesn't!'

He smiled, began to rub his thumb gently across her palm, and when she shivered, tried to pull free, his smile widened. '"The lady doth protest too much, methinks."'

Furious, embarrassed, she jerked round to face him, opened her mouth, then lamely closed it again. What could she say?

'You're a very attractive lady,' he said softly. 'And I enjoyed kissing you.'

'Is that supposed to make me feel better?' she demanded raggedly.

'Yes, because I begin now to understand the aggression. Is there a nice lady inside, Rea?'

His voice was smooth, seductive, and she felt again that alarming dip in her stomach, that frantic agitation, and his mouth was too close—very much too close. If she leant forward just a fraction... 'I don't know,' she mumbled thickly. 'I think I've forgotten who I am.'

'Be nice to find out, don't you think?'

Would it? Swallowing hard, not knowing quite how to answer, she licked dry lips. 'Why?'

'Because of an umbrella.'

'"Umbrella"?' she echoed stupidly.

'Mmm. It's in my car. Plus a small amount of lire used for a cab fare.'

Frowning, she asked, confused, 'How do you know?'

'When I went out last evening—with Claudia,' he added drily, 'an old lady was hovering on the pavement, clutching a blue umbrella and some money. She was looking for Umberto. A young lady, she said, had kindly given her the umbrella and enough money for a cab but hadn't given her the exact address so that she could return them—just Umberto's name and vague directions.'

'Oh.'

'Which, of course, is why you were late the other evening. And very wet.'

'Yes.'

'That was kind.'

'She had a little boy with her—her grandson, I think—and they were wet and cold and tired,' Rea mumbled defensively.

'And it embarrasses you to be caught out in an act of kindness?'

'No, just—it isn't anything much.' She shrugged.

'It was to her.'

Feeling awkward, she gave another small shrug.

'You have very little money—very little anything, as far as I can gather—and yet you gave all that you had to an old lady you do not know, with no guarantee that you would ever get it back—'

'It wasn't very much. Just a few lire . . .'

'When you have nothing a few lire is a great deal. And so I spent that evening trying to puzzle out the enigma that was Rea.'

'I'm not an enigma, and being nice to me is not very wise,' she added waspishly as she desperately fought a rearguard action. 'I might begin chasing you again!'

'Were you chasing me?'

'No!'

'Pity.'

'What?' she demanded in astonishment, and then heard the echo of hurrying footsteps. 'Someone's coming,' she whispered—and didn't know if she was relieved or disappointed.

He gave a wry smile, released her hand and picked up the torch he'd laid beside him on the step. And, presumably as a precautionary measure, he banged on the door.

The elderly man who opened it was profuse in his apologies, almost *bowing* to Gaetano—not that Rea understood half of what he said. She gave him a lame smile, then allowed Tano to usher her outside.

He hurried her along to his car, retrieved a rug from the back seat while she stood beside him, then wrapped her warmly in its soft folds. And then he just held her shoulders, staring down at her.

'It's stopped raining,' she said foolishly.

'Yes.'

Averting her eyes, not sure what to say to him any more, she stared up at the sky, at the stars, and gave a little shiver. 'I didn't think I would ever get out, see the sky again.'

'You think we would have left you there?' he teased gently.

'No, but it felt such a very long time.'

'It was a very long time.'

She nodded, her eyes still raised to the heavens. 'I can see Orion, the Plough—I think.' With a funny little smile on her mouth, she finally looked at him again and apologised quickly, 'I'm sorry about... I mean... Why did you say, "Pity"?' she blurted out.

He didn't answer, didn't help her out, just framed her face with his warm palms, stared down at her and smiled—a crooked smile, boyishly appealing—and she stared at him in fascination.

'Show me where you hit your head,' he ordered softly, and she obediently brushed her hair aside, showing him the bump. He traced it with a gentle finger, then lowered his head and touched his mouth to the small injury. 'All better,' he said throatily.

Her voice thick, breathing restricted, she whispered, 'Yes.' *Something* was happening but she didn't know what. He made her feel inexperienced, naïve, and because she didn't know how to flirt, play games, didn't know why he was *still* being nice she queried awkwardly, 'Did Umberto alert the church?'

He gave another wry smile. 'Mmm. Apparently when he couldn't find either of us he became worried, rang the caretaker...'

'But why did it take so long?'

'I don't know,' he replied drily. 'You can ask him when we get back. Not going to ask me why I kissed you last night?'

'What?' she asked blankly.

'You didn't think it odd?'

'Odd?'

He gave her a little shake. 'Did you really forget to give me the rest of that message?'

'Yes. Mother interrupted me just as I was going to. And then I forgot.'

'And so chased after me. Not because you wanted to see what Claudia looked like?' he teased softly.

'No! And don't smile like that! *I* don't care what she looks like! And why did you smile *then*? Because you found it funny?'

'No. I'll tell you one day—maybe.'

Feeling frustrated, out of her depth, she muttered, 'Did you smile when you'd kissed Claudia?'

'No, but then Claudia doesn't disturb me.'

Uncertain, she echoed, '"Disturb"?'

'Yes, disturb, and I don't want to be disturbed. I *never* want to be disturbed. Kissing you was a compulsion.'

'As it is with Claudia?'

'No, because Claudia never looks as though she needs to be thoroughly kissed.'

Because she already was? By him? 'And I do?' she asked faintly.

'Yes. Does Tom thoroughly kiss you?'

'No. Yes. Mind your own business.'

His smile faint, he traced one finger down her cheek, his eyes on her mouth. 'I should never have kissed you, of course. I knew that, but I never expected that it would shake my cynical soul to its roots.'

'Did it?'

'Yes. You aggravate me, irritate me, disturb—'

'The tranquillity of your days.'

'*Sì*. I had begun to wonder if there were any redeeming qualities inside that exquisite frame—and then I discovered there were, that you could be kind and generous. I had also discovered, of course, that if I dug deep enough there was also a trace of humour.'

'Up on the Palatine, do you mean?'

'Yes.'

'Then why did you say that about chasing you?' she asked confusedly.

'Because...' His smile almost self-mocking, he asked, 'You have a saying in England, don't you, something about give a man an inch and he'll take a mile?'

'Yes,' she agreed cautiously. 'You were afraid that if you were too nice to me I'd try to take advantage?'

'Something like that.'

'Because other people have?'

'Mmm.'

Claudia?

'And then I foolishly kissed you on the landing...' Tano went on.

'And insulted me again.'

'Yes, and insulted you again. And then an old lady made me feel ashamed. I missed seeing you this morning because I was away early...and then I found you in the catacombs looking lost and abandoned, vulnerable—not a way I ever expected to see you— and my apology was forgotten because I found that I wanted to kiss you again. And so I did, and got a response that tore my cynical soul right out.'

'*You* kissed *me*?'

'Mmm, as I still want to kiss you—to go on kissing you,' he murmured huskily. 'For ever and ever and ever.'

She knew that he was joking, teasing—wasn't he?— but it didn't prevent the most delicious, frightening, sensuous feeling sliding into her tummy. With a little shiver, she continued to stare up at him, a rabbit to his fox.

'And then you talked to me rationally about your problems, your animals, and I understood that the aggression stemmed from fear, worry. And now I have discovered that you are an extraordinarily vulnerable young woman—who isn't very experienced. Why do you hide yourself inside, Rea?'

Did she? Yes, she supposed she did. She refused to show weakness. And that was silly. 'I don't know,' she confessed.

'And so I discover a need in me to find out what she is like, this lady with the face of an angel.'

Lowering his head again, he touched his mouth to hers, then groaned; they both groaned, melted together, and it was like all the things she had ever imagined being in love would be, should be—warm and safe, caring, comforting, with passion lurking just below the surface of consciousness, desire building slowly, so slowly, but inexorably towards—fusion.

Her back was against the car, his body against hers, and his mouth was doing the most extraordinary things to her senses—until a car went past and he shuddered, reluctantly breaking contact.

'I'm a fool,' he said softly, eventually. 'You're cold, tired, hungry, and you need to be home in the warm. And Umberto and your mother will be frantic. Come on, let's get you back. We can continue this delightful experiment later.'

Experiment?

Moving her slightly, he opened the car door, helped her inside, then leaned down to say softly, 'It's a beautiful city, Rea; it never meant to bury you alive.'

'I know,' she agreed shakily. 'Wrong place, wrong time.'

'Yes.'

Experiment?

And when he was behind the wheel, with the heater turned up, and he was driving them back, she gazed out at a world she had for a while thought she would not see again. She pointed to the little church on their right. 'Is that Domine Quo Vadis?'

'Yes. You know what it means?'

'No.'

'"Where are you going?" Fleeing Rome to escape death at the hands of Nero's soldiers, St Peter had a vision of Christ and asked, *"Domine, quo vadis?"*—Where are you going, Lord? To which Christ replied, *"Venio iterum crucifigi,"*—I am going to be crucified again, and Peter turned back to meet his martyrdom.'

'Oh. That's lovely.'

'Yes.'

'And you love it, don't you?' she asked softly as she waved one hand to encompass the passing scenery. 'All this?'

'Yes. I find it utterly and endlessly fascinating.'

Yes. Far more than any woman would be? She didn't know. Watching until the church was out of sight, she turned her gaze toward Tano. His nose no longer looked blade-like, she decided, merely strong, and she wanted to touch him again—just a small human contact—her hand on his thigh maybe, or his arm. But he thought it was an experiment—and she didn't. She thought it was attraction.

As though aware of her need, her thoughts, he reached out, picked up her hand, held it beneath his on the wheel until they stopped near his apartment. Backing into a space, he switched off the engine,

turned, smiled at her, and reached out to frame her
dirty face in his dirty palms.

'I'm very proud of you,' he said softly.

'Are you?' she asked weakly. 'Why?'

'Because I might have expected hysteria, recriminations—and instead I got a kiss.' His tone was gentle;
he touched his mouth to hers—a light salute, an
apology, maybe—and then he gathered her close,
touched his mouth to her tangled hair.

'I don't know why it is,' he murmured humorously,
'but, dirty and dishevelled, I find you extraordinarily
fanciable.' Gazing once more into her face, he smiled.
'A beautiful lady, who could be even more beautiful
with a little gilding—and I find I have a great desire
to take you out, show you off. The Hassler, I think.
Yes? Tomorrow?'

'But that's...' she began doubtfully.

'The roof-garden restaurant?' He smiled again.
'Very expensive?'

'Yes.'

'And don't you think you deserve a treat?'

Staring into his steady grey eyes, remembering how
she was cheating him, she shook her head. 'I don't
understand you!' she blurted out.

'I know you don't. You don't know very much
about me at all.'

'Tell me.'

'In two minutes?'

'Just a little bit, then.'

'All right, just a little bit. I come from a very large
family—'

'You do?' she asked in surprise. He didn't look as
though he did. He looked singular, solitary.

'Mmm. Not siblings, but a whole army of relations—uncles, aunts, cousins—and they all have their various fingers in various pies. The odd vineyard, hotel, olive grove—that sort of thing. Property, a travel company.'

She didn't imagine that he meant an agency. And he made them sound like dirt farmers made good, which she knew very well wasn't true. Umberto had told her that he came from a very wealthy family—old money. Tano also made it sound as though he wasn't very bright and accepted any handout they might feel generous enough to give, which was even more absurd. 'Go on,' she encouraged. 'Your parents?'

'My father died when I was quite young, my mother a few years ago. Umberto is also a distant cousin, and he talked and talked about his new stepdaughter. Soon she would come, he would say. Soon. But she didn't,' he murmured in soft reproach, 'and because he is much loved, much respected—'

'You took a hand. And many invitations were extended,' she completed faintly as the truth finally hit home.

'Mmm. When he knew you were coming out he began running around in ever decreasing circles. Everything must be perfect for his Rea. Everything must run smoothly—this tour, that, lunches, dinners...'

Horrified, she stared at him aghast. 'And I... Mum said, but... Oh, Tano, he never said,' he whispered.

'No.'

'No wonder you were so...'

'Foul?' he asked helpfully.

'Yes. He doesn't know that it was you who insisted I come?'

'No.'

'And then I spoilt it all, didn't I? Going on and on about the land. Being rude...' Her eyes troubled, she searched his face. If she told him the rest, told him what she had done, he would dislike her even more—and she didn't want him to dislike her, but she did have to tell him because if he found out later... 'And so you put up with my behaviour even though you didn't like me.'

'Because I didn't *think* I liked you. But I like Umberto. And I was wrong about you, wasn't I?'

'Were you?' she asked worriedly.

'Yes.'

'How do you know? Just because I gave an old lady an umbrella... Just because when you kissed me...'

'I was disturbed? No. I mistook single-mindedness for selfishness. But I think maybe it was only thoughtlessness, hmm?'

'Yes,' she whispered again.

'And, seeing you like this, your face all dirty, your eyes frightened, I find that I don't mind at all.'

'Don't mind me being thoughtless?'

'When I'm one of the most thoughtless people I know?' he teased softly. 'No, how could I mind?'

Almost hypnotised by his soft voice, she gave a slow blink as his face moved closer, went out of focus until all the planes and angles blurred together, and then his mouth found hers in a stomach-churning kiss that left her helpless and aroused.

His long fingers spread across her ribcage beneath her raincoat, burned through her shirt. His knee touched hers—an innocent gesture that was unbearably intimate.

With a helpless little sigh she gave herself up to his warmth, his expertise, to a yearning she hadn't felt since she was eighteen—and it was spoilt because she hadn't yet told him. And because he thought that this was an experiment.

'Tano...'

Long fingers moved, touched her mouth, hushing her; grey eyes gleamed in the moonlight, smiled down into hers. Putting her own hand up to move his, she found it entangled instead, captured, carried to his mouth—a mouth that moved to the inside of her wrist, sending erotic messages to her brain, to her stomach.

'I have to talk to you,' she whispered worriedly. 'Tell you something.'

'That you love me?' He smiled.

'No,' she denied on a shocked gasp. 'How can I love you? I barely know you!'

'Only in your dreams?'

'Oh, Tano!' Was it still just a game to him? How, then, could he talk of love? 'I expect it's because of— well, because of what happened, because of the drama, the moonlight. It isn't *real*, is it?'

'Isn't it?' He moved his fingers to her jaw, held her face still, and his smile widened, teased, tormented. 'This is real,' he argued as he gathered her close again, kissed her as she had never been kissed in all of her twenty-nine years—with experience, expertise, with devastating effect. 'Isn't it?' he asked huskily.

'Yes.' Breathless, almost frightened, she stared up at him. 'What about Claudia?'

'Claudia? You think I would be kissing you like this if I wanted Claudia?'

'No. Yes. I don't know, do I?'

'Is this how you kiss Tom?'

'No!'

He chuckled. 'Why are you sounding so unbelievably shocked?'

'I'm not!'

His smile became a grin, and he hugged her close as though she was his delight. 'Stop sighing. Tired?'

'Yes, a little.' And muddled, and afraid to hope.

'And if we don't move soon we're going to take root. You're cold, shocked, and I'm getting very aroused. Kinky, huh—desiring someone who looks like a mud wrestler?'

'Do I?' But taking root sounded nice—staying here, warm and safe in his arms.

'Yes, and whilst we sit here taking our pleasure Umberto and your mother are upstairs worrying. So come on; we can talk—and love—later.'

'Yes. Tano, I truly didn't know it was your apartment. I'm sorry for—'

'You already apologised.'

'Tried!' she corrected. 'You wouldn't listen!'

'I listened,' he argued softly, 'and you're forgiven.'

'Thank you,' she said tartly, and he laughed.

'Come on.' Helping her out, he locked the car and began to help her up to the apartment.

'Why was there a doorway to nowhere?' she asked.

'A doorway to...' He frowned. 'You just lost me, I'm afraid.'

'In the trench.'

'Oh. It led to a tomb once, I assume, a long time ago before vandals, robbers and subsidence—the ancient Rome variety—got to it,' he teased. 'We discovered it by chance. All the rain we've been having washed away some topsoil and we found a marble slab—the top of the architrave. The trench was dug in order to excavate it, but sadly all we've found so far is the doorway. We'll go down a bit deeper, see if we can find anything worth salvaging.'

He smiled, hugged her against him again, and as they turned onto the last flight, as though their footsteps were being eagerly awaited, the door to the apartment was flung open and Umberto and her mother erupted out, halted, exclaimed and sighed with relief.

Her mother reached her first, hugged her, sniffed and held her off to examine her. 'Just look at you,' she complained gruffly. 'Oh, Rea.' And then Umberto was there, apologising, touching her, almost as if he was afraid that his eyes were deceiving him.

'You are all right?'

'Yes, truly. I'm fine.'

'I am so sorry. I should have waited ... It was the catacomb? Locked in?'

'Yes, but I'm all right.' Catching Tano's amused grin, she gave him a little shove, and, linking her arms with Umberto and her mother, she ushered them back inside—and then halted in shock.

'Hello, Tom,' Tom said sarcastically.

'Tom?' she queried blankly. 'What on earth are you doing here?'

'What do you think I'm doing here?' With a savagery that took her by surprise, he castigated her, 'Did you ring me? No. Did you tell me you'd moved apartments? No. Did you even tell me you'd changed telephone numbers? No! So—'

'Not *now*, Tom,' her mother put in crossly. 'Rea...'

He glared her into silence then continued, 'So, naturally worried because I could not get hold of you—and every time I tried to ring some foreigner kept yelling '*Pronto*' at me—I decided I'd better come out!

'And I have been standing in the pouring rain outside an empty apartment,' he continued even more savagely, 'for hours, getting soaking wet whilst you swan round Rome with—him! And if your mother and Umberto hadn't come to check the apartment I'd be standing there still!'

Taken aback by his fury, feeling guilty because she hadn't rung him, she whispered weakly, 'I'm sorry.'

'Are you? Well, isn't that nice? Rea is sorry! What the hell do you think you're playing at? And how in God's name did you manage to get yourself locked in a catacomb?'

'Through no fault of her own,' Umberto insisted, giving him a look of dislike as he helped Rea past him and into the lounge. Settling her in a chair, he turned once more to Tom. 'And it is not for you to reprove her; it was not her fault, not her intention to worry anyone. And she is safe now,' he added. 'That is all that matters.'

'She should have had more sense!'

'Why should she?' Tano asked, at his most relaxed, at his most dislikeable—if you were on the receiving end—his drawl more pronounced than usual as he walked across to the drinks cabinet and poured a generous amount of brandy for Rea.

'People don't go around creating scenarios in their heads just so that one day they can avoid them. At least, I don't. Would you like a drink?' he asked, punctiliously polite.

'No!'

'And I would have thought you more usefully employed thanking God that she is safe instead of reading her the Riot Act. If she were mine—'

'Well, she isn't yours! And why are you all defending her?' he demanded. 'I'm the one who's been ill used!'

'But not deliberately,' Umberto reproved. Turning to Rea, the worry returning to his eyes, he squatted beside her, rested one hand gently on her tumbled hair and asked softly, 'All right, my darling?'

Staring into his warm brown eyes, she gave a choked nod. He'd arranged all those entertainments for her, which she'd mostly spurned, and still he was kind, concerned, loving. She didn't think she deserved that sort of kindness. Reaching for his hand, she held it against her cheek. 'I love you,' she whispered. 'I'm so glad Mum found you.'

'Oh, Rea.' Looking shaken, proud, almost overcome, he squeezed her hand. 'You will be hungry, yes? Your mama has soup ready...' He straightened, smiled at Jean, and she went off to get the soup.

With a shaky sigh and an equally shaky smile Rea sipped her brandy and glanced at Tom. He looked sulky, and beside Gaetano his thin frame looked diminished. His brown hair had been cut too short; it gave him the look of a fractious schoolboy.

Spindleshanks. And no matter how much she might deny it to Tano the name did suit him. He did have thin legs—and a thin grasp of her needs. But he had come all this way to see her, and so she managed a smile for him, quietly apologised again.

'A wretched welcome for you,' she murmured.

'Yes,' he agreed stonily.

'But I don't understand why you were worried. I was coming back in a few days.'

'Were you?'

Puzzled, she frowned. 'Yes, of course. Didn't Lucy say?'

'No.'

Why not? she wondered. Because she hadn't seen him? But if she hadn't seen him ... Rubbing a hand across her forehead, trying to think, and aware of Tano listening, Rea asked cautiously, 'Isn't everything all right?'

'No, everything is not all right! You tell Lucy to move the animals, expect her to cope—and me,' he added aggrievedly, 'whilst you swan round Rome having a really nice time! Did you think *I* would take them?'

'No, of course not.'

'Then who?'

'I don't know!' she cried. 'There must be somewhere! And I'm coming back on Monday!'

'Meanwhile someone else has to make your decisions! I couldn't get you on the phone! Lucy couldn't get you on the phone—'

Yes, she could.

'—and you seem to forget that I have a practice to run!'

'I don't forget—haven't forgotten,' she returned, beginning to feel muddled and confused, tired and shivery again. 'But I didn't know what else to do!'

'Well, doesn't *that* make a change?' he retorted sarcastically. 'Usually you can't *wait* to tell everybody what to do!'

'No,' she denied, with a frown.

'Yes! And you're the one who couldn't be bothered to get in touch! Once, you rang me—when you arrived. "I'll be back in a few days," you said! And when I do arrive, go out of my way to find out what on earth you're up to, you're out swanning around the catacombs with *him*!'

'I wasn't—'

'Oh, no?' he sneered.

'No!'

'And then you come out with some cock-and-bull story about being locked in!'

'I was locked in!'

'Well, whether you were or you weren't, do you have any idea the trouble you've put everyone to?'

'Stop it,' Umberto said quietly, but with a definite note of authority in his voice. 'Is no trouble for Rea. Is never any trouble for Rea.'

Surprised, she glanced at him, and her eyes filled with tears. 'Thank you,' she whispered, and to her horror found that she couldn't stop crying. She felt Tano's hand descend onto her shoulder and exert gentle, comforting pressure.

'Enough,' Tano said quietly, but with a great deal more authority than Umberto. 'Now is not the time for post-mortems. There is a small hotel a few doors down. Book yourself in; you can use my name.'

'I don't need to use your name!'

'Then use your own,' Tano argued indifferently, 'but use it now.'

'No!' Tom exploded. 'What is this—a third-rate melodrama? I've been insulted, ignored, barely greeted—by anyone! I'm jet lagged, and all you can talk about is—'

'You do not get jet lag on a two-hour flight,' Rea put in. 'Don't be ridiculous!'

'Me, ridiculous? And he isn't, I suppose?' he derided, with a sick glance at Tano. '*He* was the one who wouldn't rent you the land! He's the one who obviously doesn't mind that you put your damned animals on it anyway!'

'*No!*' No! she wanted to howl, Not now, not yet.

The hand on her shoulder stilled, was removed. 'What?' Tano asked softly—so softly, yet with more impact than any of Tom's shouting. You could have heard a pin drop. 'What?' he repeated.

CHAPTER FIVE

Tom looked at Tano then at Rea, and a look of shock spread over his face. 'You didn't tell him, did you?'

Feeling sick, she glanced at Umberto and her mother, who stood in the doorway holding a tray; she saw the shock on their faces. Glanced back at Tano and saw—nothing. 'Tano—' she began.

'*Gae*tano,' he corrected her, and his voice was cold, distant, all warmth withdrawn. His eyes were on Tom, but he was talking to her. 'Is this true?'

'Yes. But—'

'You moved your animals onto my land?'

'Yes,' she whispered.

'Without asking, without permission. Dogs?'

'Dogs?' She frowned. 'No, I didn't want to take in any more when Ralph died until I knew what the outcome was going to be, and the few I was still boarding I found room for in another kennels. It was only the wildlife.'

'I see,' he stated icily. 'And your camper?'

'In the barn,' she confessed miserably. 'I tried to tell you!' she burst out. 'But I couldn't seem to find the opportunity!'

'In six days?' he asked silkily.

'No. Yes. I didn't think you'd *mind*!'

'Didn't you?'

'No. I thought you'd agree! It wouldn't have made any difference to you... Sorry,' she muttered, subsiding. 'But don't shout at me. Please don't shout at me.'

'I wasn't shouting. I never do.'

'Well, there's no need to sound so *proud* about it!' she exclaimed woefully.

'Pardon?'

'Nothing.'

He gave a derisive little inclination of his head—cold derision, not mocking or amused. 'And if I'd agreed, I would never have known, would I?'

'No. I'm sorry.'

'Are you? It all makes a rather bizarre sort of sense now, doesn't it?'

'What does?'

'Your behaviour.'

'My...?' Horrified, she said, 'You don't think I—?'

'Yes. I rather think I do. First there was aggression, then an apology, then...' With a dismissive look which hurt more than words might have done he began to walk away.

'Tano!'

He halted, turned, and, his face a study in marble, corrected icily, '*Gae*tano. And first thing in the morning you will ring your assistant and get everything moved. Otherwise *I* will sue.' Opening his bedroom door, he walked inside and closed it quietly behind him.

'Oh, Rea,' her mother said softly.

'I didn't think he'd mind,' she repeated almost blankly. And he surely couldn't think...? Not that she'd...? Catching Tom's continuing look of shock, she looked quickly away.

'I don't know you at all, do I?' he asked reprovingly.

'No,' she mumbled.

'I didn't think you would *ever* do something like that! And you've implicated me, haven't you?'

'No.'

'Yes, you have. By association. Does Lucy know?'

'No,' she mumbled again.

'So she's a dupe too.'

'Yes. No.' Raking a hand tiredly through her hair, she said quietly, 'I'm sorry. For everything. But what else could I do? *You* wouldn't have them . . .'

'Don't blame your behaviour on me.'

'No. Sorry.' Looking up at him, her face sad, she added, 'I always tried to tell you that I wasn't the person you thought. Not that I cheated—lied,' she added honestly, 'but I'm not—'

'Nice?' he asked.

'Is nice,' Umberto insisted fiercely. 'She was worried for her animals. Is understandable.'

Giving him a grateful smile, she argued, 'No, Umberto, it wasn't nice. It was a stupid thing to have done.'

'Criminal,' Tom substituted, still looking unbelievably betrayed. 'I thought I loved you. I asked you to be my wife.'

The greatest accolade. Don't be bitchy, Rea, she told herself. 'Oh, Tom,' she cried wearily, 'I always told you I wouldn't marry you, that I wasn't in love with you. Don't make it sound as though I misled you. I'm sorry you had a wasted journey, sorry you had to hang around in the rain. It never even occurred to me that you would come, never occurred to me that Lucy wouldn't explain.'

And why hadn't she? Rea wondered. Because she'd forgotten? Hadn't had time? Was that why she'd sounded evasive? Because she'd forgotten to tell Tom? And why, really, had Tom come at all?

'What will you do now?' she asked him quietly. 'There aren't any available seats on a flight until Monday.'

'I'm sure I'll manage,' he said stiffly. With a nod to Umberto and her mother, he picked up his suitcase which rested by the wall, and let himself out.

Umberto closed the door behind him, turned to look at Rea, sighed. 'I am sorry. If you wish for him to stay...'

'No, I don't want him to stay.'

'You are tired,' he added gently. 'Still shocked, perhaps. Have your soup.'

'What? No. I have to talk to Ţano. Excuse me,' she muttered hastily. Discarding the rug and the raincoat, she hurried out and along to Tano's room. She didn't bother to knock, just walked in. The fact that he was in the bathroom—in the shower—didn't even register at first, and when it did she thought she was too tired to care. Pulling open the shower door, she turned off the water.

'What do you mean it makes a "bizarre sort of sense"?' she asked numbly. 'You can't really think...?'

He grabbed her arm and shoved her backwards, all the way into the bedroom. 'Do not,' he gritted, 'ever come into my room uninvited! Now get out!'

Shocked by his violence, she stubbornly shook her head. 'No. I want to know what you meant! You think I got myself locked in the catacombs on purpose? Arranged for you to rescue me? Well, do you? Hurled myself into your arms from some great master plan? You think I was *that* calculating? That desperate?'

'Weren't you? Not even for your precious animals? What were you willing to give for my agreement—sex? A quick tumble on the bed?'

'No! Don't be disgusting!'

'And what did you promise Tom that he needs to rush out here to see what you're up to?'

'I didn't promise him anything!'

'Kisses for foxes?'

'No! None of it was premeditated! Bressingham threw me off the land and I had nowhere to go! I *tried* but I couldn't find anywhere! And it wouldn't have hurt you to let me use it! I wasn't doing any damage! I only put up a few sheds, used the barn!'

'*Are* using the barn!' he corrected coldly. 'And how would you like it if someone moved into your garden uninvited?'

'I'd find out the facts first!'

'Would you? Would you really? The way you found out the facts about me? Playboy? Womaniser?'

'I did not say you were a womaniser!'

'Implied it!'

'No, I didn't!' Swinging away, she hurried to the door. He grabbed her, hauled her back.

'Oh, no,' he said derisively. 'You don't run out just when it's getting interesting!'

'It is not getting interesting,' she protested thickly. 'And go and put some clothes on!'

'Why? Bother you, does it?'

'No!' But it did. It was beginning to bother her very badly.

'No, I didn't think it would.'

'What does that mean?'

'Exactly what it implies.'

'That I'm some sort of...? Well, thank you very much!'

Both breathing hard, they stared at each other, and it was Rea who gave in first. Miserably aware that it was all her own fault, wanting so much to be held, comforted, to make him understand, so very aware of the wet, naked body in front of her, the slick skin, the hand still holding her arm, wanting to touch, feel, she whispered, 'Stalemate. Oh, Tano, I didn't...'

'Didn't you?' he asked bitterly. Dragging her against him, he stared down into her eyes, and then kissed her, hard. Too hard. With deliberation, anger, hatred almost, and then he shoved her away. 'And if you'd asked me, explained properly in the first place, you think I would have left you with no alternative? I did not know Bressingham's brother had already thrown you off.'

'I know.'

'Then why not tell me?'

'Because you wouldn't *listen*! You were so busy castigating me for neglecting Umberto and Mother—'

'Don't make excuses!'

'I'm not, but... And what did you mean about the dogs?'

'Artefacts, pottery shards—dogs dig things up!'

'Oh. I see.'

'Good.'

'But there aren't any dogs.'

'No, but *I* didn't know that, did I?'

'No,' she whispered miserably.

'No. Now get out.'

She fled. Avoiding both her mother's and Umberto's concerned faces, she ran into her room and shut the door. Throwing herself across the bed, she hugged the pillow tight.

'Rea?'

'Not now, Mum,' she mumbled. 'We'll talk in the morning.' She heard her mother sigh, her low voice as she said something to Umberto, and then the sound of their footsteps and the closing of their bedroom door.

Her mouth hurt, she thought bleakly, and scrubbed it across the pillow. No more kisses. A lesson learned. And she only had herself to blame, although had he really needed to be quite so self-righteous about it all?

Staring blindly at the wall, she eventually stirred herself, stripped off and went to have a bath. She would leave in the morning, camp out at the airport or something. She couldn't stay here. And she was running out of things to wear.

Feeling wrung out, empty, knowing that she was incapable of making any more decisions that night, she went to bed, and if she dreamed she didn't remember any of it when she woke, but there was a great big ache inside her—an ache she didn't know how to dissolve.

The apartment was silent when she emerged from her room. Empty. She didn't know where Tano had gone, but there was a note from her mother in the kitchen to say that she and Umberto were transferring their things back to their apartment. They'd be back about noon. Why were they moving back? Because of her? Because they now felt they couldn't stay in Tano's apartment after her behaviour? Well, she couldn't leave without seeing them, and didn't want to leave without seeing Tano, because she couldn't quite believe that he wouldn't forgive her. But before breakfasting, before packing, she must ring Lucy.

She heard him come in an hour later—an hour in which everything had changed. Pacing back and forth, worried, perplexed, frightened, every muscle taut, she waited for Lucy to ring back. Hearing footsteps behind her, knowing instinctively who it was, she stiffened. Expecting further recriminations, she got in first.

'No more,' she said quietly, even though he hadn't spoken. 'Please, no more. Not now.' Turning to face him, she continued earnestly, 'I truly didn't cheat you deliberately. It wasn't premeditated. I did try to find something else, and when I couldn't I thought... Well, it doesn't matter now. I just wanted you to know that I didn't...in the catacombs...' He didn't answer, didn't move, and so she ploughed on, 'I know I handled it all wrong, but, oh, Tano—'

'Gaetano,' he corrected.

'Don't,' she cried. 'Please don't. I didn't...' Hands clenched tight at her sides, she continued to stare at him, a plea in her eyes that he ignored.

'Didn't...?' he asked, his voice flat without inflexion. 'Didn't what? Chase me? Pursue me? You accused me of being calculating, but how much more calculating were you?'

'I *wasn't*!' She extended one hand out toward him, then let it drop limply to her side. 'I wasn't,' she repeated numbly.

'Weren't you?' he asked bitingly.

'No. And now they've disappeared,' she said uselessly. 'Gone. Where could they have gone?' Shoving her hair back, an expression of fearful bewilderment in her eyes, she repeated, 'Gone. Lucy went this morning—and they weren't there! Who would have taken them? And why? Bressingham? Do you think he could have taken them?'

'Taken *what*?' Tano demanded wrathfully.

'The animals!'

'The ani—' A look of disgusted enlightenment spread over his face, and, swearing under his breath, he turned on his heel and snatched up the hall phone. He punched out numbers whilst Rea stared at him in blank astonishment; she tried to gain his attention.

'Who are you ringing? Bressingham?' How would he know Bressingham's number? 'Tano!'

He waved her off impatiently, spoke briefly with someone in English, asked tersely if they had her animals, then replaced the receiver.

'Was that Bressingham? Does he have them?'

'Of course Bressingham doesn't have them. Don't be ridiculous!'

'Then who does?'

'Tom!' Mouth tight, he muttered something, then exploded savagely, 'What I did not tell him to do was take them *now*! *Or* without telling your assistant!'

'Tom?' she repeated blankly. 'How could Tom have them? Tom's here!'

'Tom is not here. Tom is in England!'

'But he *can't* be! There aren't any flights!'

'I had him flown back,' he said tersely.

'You? How could you have had him flown back?'

'Because a member of my family owns a charter service! After I had—spoken with you last night,' he resumed, more moderately, 'I walked down to the hotel, saw Tom. We talked, and no matter what I might think of you personally I will not be deliberately responsible for the ill-treatment of animals—*any* animals. As a short-term measure Tom is housing them at the practice. For a fee,' he added, with a distasteful twist to his mouth.

'For a... You *paid* him to take them, deliberately went behind my back? Arbitrarily arranged the transportation of *my* animals...? Colluded with Tom...? How dare you? I've been worried sick! Sick!' she repeated. 'Lucy is frantic, blaming herself... and all the while... How *dare* you?'

'How dare I?' he queried coldly. 'How *dare* I? I think I've been remarkably restrained about the whole distasteful episode. And there would have been no need for Lucy to be frantic if Tom had followed my instructions.'

'Followed *your* instructions?' she spat. 'They're *my* animals! And they weren't hurting anything! It would have waited until I got back on Monday.'

'I *know* it would have waited,' he grated, 'and I did not tell him to take them *now*. But in case it has slipped your memory it is *my* land they were residing on!'

'Causing no harm at all!'

'Which is beside the point!'

'No, it isn't! I don't *want* Tom to have my animals!'

'Then go and tell him so! Go and make your own arrangements! Now!'

'I will! As soon as Umberto and Mum get back. And no, I shall not need a lift to the airport! Goodbye—*Gae*tano,' she emphasised.

He made an angry sort of hissing sound between his teeth, swung away, and she heard his rapid footsteps along the hall, then the slam of the front door. Bitter fury ravaging her face, she slammed her hand against the wall, then had to clamp her mouth tight to stop the stupid quiver of her lower lip. She didn't *want* Tom to have them, she thought petulantly. And now she'd have to ring Lucy, explain, put *her* mind at rest.

Ignoring Lucy's bewilderment, half-formed sentences and queries, Rea told her tersely what had happened, then stalked along to her room to finish her packing. Slumping tiredly onto the edge of the bed, she put her head in her hands. 'No matter what I might think of you,' he had said ... And she should have thanked him, shouldn't she? Not railed at him like a fishwife. But she'd been frightened ... More excuses.

Her sigh had a defeated sound to it as she waited for her parents to return. Waited and waited.

Oh, where the devil were they? Glancing at her watch again, seeing that it was still only five minutes after she'd last looked, she trailed into the lounge, pulled back the curtain to stare down into the street. The traffic at the end of the road was snarled up, she saw, and in the distance there was a column of smoke—kids burning rubbish, perhaps, or a bonfire in the park—but her thoughts were absent, unconnected.

At least the animals were safe. For the moment. But to high-handedly... And what had Tom been paid? Was she supposed to continue the payment?

With another deep sigh, not wanting to think about either Tano or Tom, restless and impatient, she stared once more along the street, prayed for the sight of Umberto's blue car. Oh, come on, come on, she silently urged; I want to go before Gaetano comes back.

How *could* he think she'd kissed him because...? Well, she'd pay him back, every wretched penny—or lire. Perhaps she could sell her camper; there might be enough left over to pay off some of her other debts. Perhaps she would give up looking after animals, become a sales rep or something, come out to Rome, stay with Umberto and her mother for a while, make up for her recent behaviour.

But if she did that she would see Gaetano, wouldn't she? Was bound to. No more kisses, she thought bleakly. She would never now know what he was like as a lover. What *was* he like? Inventive, she guessed, and, as though her thoughts had conjured him up, she saw his car pull up. Sloppy parking, she thought, and he didn't even lock his door, just slammed it to and almost ran into the doorway below her.

Tano never ran—the same way he never shouted. Had he had second thoughts? Come to say he forgave her? She didn't know if she wanted to be forgiven now. Not after the way he'd behaved, the fright he had given her.

She heard the front door open, and slowly released the curtain, let it fall back into place. Turning to face the doorway, her body tense, she waited, but when he appeared all thoughts of forgiveness fled. He looked grey, sick. 'Tano?' she whispered, and a cold little finger of fear slid down her spine. 'What is it? What's happened? Are you ill?'

'No,' he managed, and his voice was quiet, serious, but no longer angry. 'Rea...'

'What? What is it?' she demanded urgently. Hurrying toward him, she halted barely a hand's breadth away, stared into his white face, felt her heart kick and jerk, her breath stop. 'What?'

He grasped her hands and held them very tight. 'Rea... Oh, sweet God, Rea, there's been an accident.'

'Accident? Are you hurt?' Swiftly checking him over with her eyes, she barely registered his denial.

'No, not me. Not me,' he repeated, and for a moment sounded so anguished, so—desperate that she jerked in fright.

'You hit someone? Someone ran out?'

'No.' He briefly closed his eyes, snatched a quick breath, and said quietly, 'Umberto and...'

'Umberto?' she queried sickly. 'And Mother?' Disbelieving, unable to take it in, she just stared at him. 'Accident? In the car?'

'Yes.'

'Bad?'

He nodded.

As she tried to free her hands in order to run towards his car, go to them, Tano halted her, refused to release her.

'We have to go!'

'Yes, in a moment.'

'No, now.'

'Listen,' he urged. 'Please, just listen.'

She felt the breath he dragged into his lungs, squinched her eyes tight shut, didn't want to listen, know, believe.

'Someone going too fast swerved out of line, hit Umberto's car, pushed it into the path of a lorry. It—they... We managed to get them out, and they've been taken to the hospital, but they...' Closing his eyes for a minute, still able to see the blood, the awful injuries, he squeezed her hands tight. 'I don't think Umberto's too bad, but your mother... I just need to warn you that she...'

'Oh, dear God,' she whispered raggedly. 'But she is alive? Truly?'

'Yes. But there was a fire...'

'Fire?' she repeated numbly, not sure how she was managing to hang onto her sanity.

'Yes.'

The column of smoke she had seen. Not kids burning rubbish. Her parents...

'But I don't think the burns are too bad. We got her out before—'

'We? You were there?'

'Yes.'

'That was lucky,' she said stupidly.

'Lucky?' he asked, and for a moment he sounded incredibly bitter.

Not understanding, she glanced down at his hands, sucked in her breath at the sight of the angry blisters on his knuckles. 'Oh, Tano.'

'It's all right. We'll go now, yes?'

She nodded. She went as she was, her mind scurrying uselessly as she tried to imagine the worst. Tano had tried to prepare her, so it must be bad—but so long as they lived... Were they badly burned, was that what he'd been trying to say?

Automatically halting beside his car, she stared blankly at the front wing, and only gradually registered the damage. Bent and buckled, traces of blue paint...

Snapping up her head, she stared at him as he opened her door. It was him. He was the one who'd hit them. That was why he'd sounded bitter. Oh, dear God, he'd slammed out of the apartment, angry, driven off in a temper, met Umberto and her mother coming back...

But how could she say it? How could she accuse him? He must be feeling... And then they were at the hospital and he was hurrying her along endless corridors, asking questions, directions. Still numb, unable to take in anything, she halted when he halted at the nurses' station, stared at the young nurse, watched her mouth move as she conversed with Tano, and seemed incapable of registering anything.

'Your mother's still in surgery,' he said quietly. 'We have to wait.'

'Umberto?'

'Still being cleaned up.'

She nodded, allowing him to lead her to a small lounge—a lounge she was to get to know very well over the next few days.

'The nurse will bring you a cup of tea,' he told her quietly. 'I have some telephone calls I need to make. You'll be all right?'

She nodded jerkily, not taking anything in. Hands clasped tightly in her lap, she prayed to any god that might be listening, and then, what felt like a lifetime later, they were allowed to see Umberto.

'He looks so old,' she whispered as she stared down at a face no longer ruddy. He looked grey, crumpled, his greying hair all untidy, and she wanted to comb it, make him look nice. Eyes flooding with tears, she bit back a sob.

'He'll be all right,' Tano said quietly, but he didn't sound any more convinced than she felt, although they had been assured that he was in no danger.

The nurse said something and Tano translated. 'A broken wrist, cuts and bruises, mild concussion. He's sedated. Won't come round until morning.' He took her arm and led her outside, and then—then they were allowed to see her mother who was in Intensive Care.

'They should be together,' she said emptily. 'When he wakes and Mother isn't there—'

'Yes,' he agreed heavily.

Intensive Care was a frightening place—all white, sterile, bleeping monitors, tubes. There was so much equipment, and, in the middle of it, her mother. Her head was bandaged, her lip split, and she looked sunken and frail, so very small.

'Oh, Mum,' Rea whispered helplessly. One small hand lay outside the covers, the other was hidden in bandages that extended to her shoulder. A cage rested across her legs beneath the blanket; and Rea closed her eyes for a moment and swayed. Tano caught her, held her against him as he too stared down at her mother.

'What's wrong with her?' Rea asked.

He quietly repeated the question to the nurse, then explained, 'Head injuries, both legs broken, left arm and side—burned.'

Looking up at him, seeing the anguish on his face, she looked quickly away. 'It was you, wasn't it?' she asked, her voice barely audible. 'You pushed your car into theirs.'

'Yes. And you couldn't blame me any more than I blame myself. I took a chance...' A high-pitched tone like a car alarm suddenly broke the silence and they both froze. The nurse leapt into action, shoved them outside, pressed the panic button, and within seconds people were racing from everywhere, or so it seemed.

Standing in the corridor, her hand clenched on Tano's arm, she stood in rigid shock. 'If she dies...'

'Don't... Dear God, don't.'

'It's your fault. It's your *fault*!' she cried.

'You think I don't know that? You think I haven't been running it over and over in my head, wanting to make it different? Wishing...' Turning away, he walked to the end of the corridor, stared from the end window, his back rigid.

Yes, of course he had, and she hadn't meant to accuse him. Wishing the words unsaid, wanting to go to him, hold him, she bit her lip, leaned back against the wall, stared with anxious eyes at the door of her mother's room—and all she could think was that now she would never have a chance to make it up to her, be the daughter she wanted. And what would Umberto do without his lovely Jean?

Face wet with tears that she didn't know she was shedding, exhaustion and tension making her feel faint, Rea waited for what felt like hours, and then the door opened and a doctor gave her a cautious smile.

'She's all right?' she whispered fearfully.

He said something she didn't understand, frustratedly shoved his glasses back up his nose and tried again. She called frantically to Tano. He turned, strode back.

'I don't know what he's saying!'

He spoke quickly with the doctor, then nodded, gave a long sigh. 'She's stable. Tonight and tomorrow will be the testing time. He says you may sit with her for a while.'

'Yes. Thank you,' she said dazedly to the doctor. '*Grazie. Molte grazie.*'

'*Prego.*' He smiled, patted her hand in a fatherly gesture, then turned back to Tano and said something else. He saw his hands, tutted, caught his arm and led him away.

The nurse came to collect her, and, walking on unsteady legs into the room, Rea collapsed into the chair that had been set for her.

She stayed there all night, refused to go back to the apartment, frightened that if she removed her concentration for even a moment something would happen.

She wouldn't even leave her mother the next morning to visit Umberto. Tano did that and came quietly to report on his progress. She glanced at his bandaged knuckles, then looked quickly away.

By five o'clock they'd pronounced her mother out of immediate danger, and reluctantly Rea allowed herself to be taken back to the flat for a shower, a change of clothes, something to eat. But she wouldn't sleep, wanted only to get back to the hospital.

She didn't know what to say to Tano, didn't know how to unsay what she had said, and in the end said nothing. And that was wrong because she knew that he was suffering as much as she—possibly more because it had been his fault—but the words to absolve him would not come.

For the whole of that nightmare week, barely sleeping, snatching only catnaps, Rea kept vigil. Her mother was awake for some of the time, but seemed confused, dopey—and Umberto just seemed lost until her mother was moved from Intensive Care and into a side-ward with her husband. And from then, that little turning-point, Rea knew that they would both recover.

She didn't feel as though she would. She felt wrung out, fragile, and she ought to go home. Tano had rung Lucy, explained, and there was no immediate rush, she supposed; Lucy would look after the animals as well as she herself would. And she was still reluctant to leave in case of set-backs—although she'd been assured they wouldn't happen, and that soon, when her mother was stronger, she would be transferred to another hospital for skin grafts to her burned arm and side.

'They need rest and quiet, some sunshine—and so do you,' the doctor told her through Tano. 'Go away.'

As Tano drove her back to the apartment Rea thought about the doctor's words, and, knowing that if she didn't get away, she was the one who would crack up, she said quietly, 'I think I'll take the doctor's advice—

go away for a few days before returning to England. I'll come back, of course, when Mum has to have her grafts, but...'

His voice equally quiet, sombre, Tano advised, 'Go to the lake.'

'The lake?'

'Yes, there's a villa there.'

'Yours?'

'The—family's,' he explained after a tiny pause. 'It will be quiet, restful. You would be very welcome to use it.'

'By myself?'

'If that's what you'd like.'

'Yes,' she agreed eagerly, 'by myself, just until...' Peace and quiet, no need to think, worry. She could sleep away her exhaustion, get away from Tano for a while, from her feelings of guilt at the way she was treating him, unable to be natural. There were so many constraints between them—the row over the animals, the accident, accusations. 'Could I go today? Now?'

He nodded, looked as though he was about to say something, then sighed. 'I'll ring through as soon as we get to the apartment, get someone to stock up for you, and after you're showered and changed, had something to eat, we'll go. All right?'

She nodded. 'You won't mind driving me?'

'No.'

He'd seemed remote and formal since the accident, as though she were a stranger. Because he was still blaming himself? Or because he disliked her, could not forgive her for her deceit? Did he still think that she had pursued him deliberately? With so much else on her mind she hadn't had time to think about it.

Perhaps she could do so at the lake, for whatever difference thinking might make.

The villa was tucked into the hillside, and from her bedroom window she could see the lake. It looked green, mystical, and if she looked the other way she could see the top of Castel Gandolfo, the summer residence of the Pope.

'There's a small village,' Tano explained from behind her, 'and plenty of shops for you to potter in if you feel up to it. There's a restaurant, a café, and someone will come in to clean, cook your meals; she won't intrude,' he added quickly. 'She understands some English, so speak or not, as you want. She won't be offended. Her name's Sylvia. You'll be all right?'

Rea nodded, only wanting him to go.

'And if you should need me...anything,' he substituted, 'I've left numbers where I can be reached beside the phone.'

She nodded again, impatient now to be alone, and his face tightened as if in pain.

'Look after yourself,' he said gruffly, and then, thankfully, he left.

During the first two days, Rea did very little; she either sat on the terrace, stared out over the lake, or went for long rambling walks, deliberately keeping her mind empty of everything.

But gradually, as proper meals and sleep healed body and mind, as energy returned, she allowed herself to think about all that had happened, began to feel wretched about accusing Tano. It had been so very unfair. And she didn't blame him, not really. Certainly Umberto and her mother didn't.

She was such a tough lady, everyone had always thought, or said—aggressive, someone who knew what she wanted and went out to get it. And it was a lie. At the first test she had gone to pieces. No, that had been the second test. She had gone to pieces in the catacombs too, hadn't she? And now perhaps she needed to reassess herself, come to terms with her weakness. It wasn't a crime, it wasn't even shameful, but she had always assumed that she would cope better with drama.

If Umberto's sister walked in right now, Rea didn't think she would recognise her, or any of the other relations who had come to the hospital. And that was shaming.

Tano was the one who'd coped, who'd been there whenever she'd needed him to translate, fill in forms, and she'd taken it all for granted. And now she needed to thank him, apologise. Things would never be quite the same as before, but the gods had been kind. Her mother and Umberto would be well again, and if there was now an ache in her heart for a promise that would never be fulfilled, for a loving closeness with Tano— well, she would have to learn to live with it.

She tried to ring him the next morning, felt disappointed and empty when his phone remained unanswered. Replacing the receiver, hovering indecisively, she finally went for a walk.

Staring out over the village, she debated going down for a coffee, having a look round the shops, then changed her mind. She'd try ringing him again, keep trying until she reached him. Eager now, feeling more decisive, she hurried back—and saw him standing on the terrace looking out over the lake.

With a wide smile, she quickened her pace, then sobered, came to a halt, almost afraid to approach in case...in case he wasn't pleased to see her. She remembered his formality, the way he carefully hadn't touched her. Because of the land? Because of how she'd been?

He was wearing a short-sleeved blue shirt and jeans, his tall frame stooped, hands gripping the rail in front of him, and as she watched he straightened, turned his head.

She half raised her hand to wave, then aborted the gesture. Perhaps he'd come to tell her that her time was up, that the family needed the villa for themselves. And if he hadn't moved, roused her from her introspection, she'd maybe have stood there all afternoon.

Stepping down from the terrace, he began walking towards her, and she finally managed to unglue her feet. They met a few yards from the villa, stared at each other almost assessingly, and Rea felt awkward, constrained, with no knowledge at all of what to say.

Looking down, she scuffed her toe in the dust. 'Hello,' she greeted quietly.

'Rea,' he answered formally. 'How are you?'

'Fine.'

'You look better.'

'Yes.' Forcing herself to look at him, she blurted out, 'Ta— Gaetano—'

'Tano,' he corrected quietly.

'What?'

'Tano.'

'But you said—'

'Altogether too much. Tano's fine.'

'Oh.' Searching his eyes, she had a sudden vivid flashback of him naked, wet from his shower, holding her, his skin gleaming, and she looked quickly away. 'I'm sorry,' she whispered.

'For what?'

'Accusing you. And I didn't thank you for making all the arrangements, for translating...'

'You don't need to thank me. I love them too.'

'Yes, I know. And I didn't mean to blame you; it was an accident.'

'No,' he denied, 'it was a calculated risk. I might have killed them.'

'Risk?' Frowning, she stared at him in confusion. 'Risk?'

'Yes. It might not have worked. If I had left well alone the car might not have caught fire.'

Her frown deeper, she queried, 'Left well alone? I don't understand what you mean.'

Searching her face, it was his turn to frown. 'If I hadn't shunted the car away from the lorry.'

'*Away* from? I thought you shunted the car *into* the lorry.'

'You thought *I* caused the accident?'

'Yes. You said... And your wing was all buckled...' And yet Umberto had said, 'If it hadn't been for Tano...risking his life... Crazy thing to do.' She'd thought he'd meant rescuing her mother from the car. 'Tell me,' she said faintly.

The frown still in his eyes, he explained slowly, 'A car shunted Umberto into the path of a lorry. It caught the front bumper, turned the car over and, because of the angle at which it hit, its momentum was beginning to swing the rear of the car into the path of its wheels. I drove across the intersection, aimed my car at the rear of Umberto's and smashed it free. Unfortunately, the friction or a spark from something else set the spilled petrol alight...'

'Oh, my God,' she whispered in horror. 'You could have been killed.'

He shrugged.

'And I thought...'

'That I had caused the accident?'

'Yes. Oh, Tano, I'm so sorry. But you were so... And when I asked you didn't deny it.'

'I could have killed them,' he said quietly.

'But if you hadn't done that the lorry would have—' Breaking off, she swallowed hard because she could see it all so clearly now. Even braking, the lorry would have rolled right over the top of them. 'If you hadn't they would have been killed anyway. Wouldn't they?'

'So I thought at the time. But with hindsight...'

Tentatively touching his arm, she felt the bunching of the muscles, and not knowing if it was because of her touch or memories of the accident, she slowly withdrew her hand. When he'd come to the flat to tell her he must still have been in shock, pain... 'I'm so sorry.'

'An understandable error.'

'No, I should have made sure. I tried to ring you this morning,' she added quietly.

'Did you?'

'Yes. To apologise, to thank you... Do your relatives need the villa back? Is that why you came?'

'No. I came to see how you were.'

'Oh. Are you—er—staying for a while?'

'If you'd like me to.'

'Yes, yes, I'd like that.'

We sound so stilted, she thought, like strangers; and she wanted to hold him, be held, to touch her mouth to his, to have everything how it had been before. Snatching in a funny little breath, she gave him a bright smile. 'Have you eaten?'

'No.'

She nodded, led the way back to the villa. Sylvia was there and Tano smiled at her, spoke with her in Italian, and Rea felt awkward again, like an unwanted guest.

They lunched on the terrace, made silly, meaningless small talk until even that petered out, and she apologised again. 'I'm sorry, I'm not very good at small talk. I don't think I've ever, you know, just passed the time of day.'

'It doesn't matter.'

'No.' But it did, and she felt stupid, inadequate— and she had never ever felt like that before. 'I didn't even ask after your hands. Are they all right?'

Glancing down, absently examining the shiny red skin across the backs of his knuckles, he flexed his fingers. 'Yes. They're fine.'

She nodded. 'I'll get Sylvia to make up your bed,' she added abruptly, and fled inside.

By the following day it was worse. Communication seemed impossible. She was too tense, and he was abrupt then apologetic, and the stupid thing was that she couldn't remember how she had used to behave with him.

After a virtually silent lunch she made an excuse that she needed something from the village and hastily escaped. She got halfway down the track, then halted, staring despairingly at nothing. This could go on for days, and she wouldn't be able to stand it. If they didn't talk . . . Turning, she hurried back to the villa, found him in his room.

He was packing, shoving things angrily into his grip.

CHAPTER SIX

'YOU'RE leaving?' Rea asked in frightened disbelief.

'Yes,' Tano agreed tersely, his back to her.

'But why?'

'Why?' he demanded, with a hollow laugh. Hands stilling, he suddenly clenched them and swung to face her. 'Because I really can't take any more.'

'"Can't take any more"?' she echoed weakly. 'Of me?'

'Yes! Of wanting you! Of trying to keep my hands to myself, or taking cold showers! Of feeling . . . Oh, to hell with it!' Reaching out, he dragged her toward him, against him, stared into her wide eyes, then began to kiss her with a hunger that first shocked her then found an answering aggression.

He shoved his bag off the bed, dragged her down, rolled to cover her, continued to kiss her with a need that transcended sense, with an explosive release from tension.

Feeling feverish, desperate for human warmth—*his* human warmth—she kissed him back, held him as though she would never let him go again.

'I want to hold you naked in my arms,' he insisted thickly against her neck. 'Want an end to this anguish.'

'Anguish?' She shivered.

'Yes! Feeling stupid and helpless, unable to alleviate your pain, not knowing what to do to make it better.'

'It is better.'

'Now, yes, but no thanks to me.' Raising his head, he groaned, 'It was *destroying* me to see how you were!' Angry and helpless, pushing her tumbled hair back, his hands rough, he stared into her startled eyes, and now—now she could see the Italian passion, not the English self-containment, a man of warm blood, not cool calculation.

'It wasn't your fault...' she began as her hands automatically soothed him, wandered at will over his strong back, able at last to feel the muscles, the tendons.

'Wasn't it? Your mother said Tom had no generosity of spirit; what generosity did I have?' he demanded. 'You were shaken, hurt, frightened after the catacombs; what did I do? Split hairs, accuse, as though I were a perfect human being, infallible!'

His eyes were bright, piercing, full of self-denigration, and words, half in English, half in Italian, hot, passionate, full of pain, self-disgust, continued to spill from him as though they'd been dammed up. She stared at him in bewildered astonishment.

'Stop, oh, stop,' she cried. Holding him, aching for him, for herself, she pleaded, 'No more. You weren't at fault, never at fault; it was only my arrogance. And what about me? Blaming you? *Accusing* you! *That's* been haunting me!'

'Has it?'

'Yes! You made all the arrangements, informed everyone. I didn't do anything,' she finished on a little whisper of shame. 'If it hadn't been for you—'

'If it hadn't been for me,' he completed grimly, 'you might not have had to go through all that trauma! I wanted to hold you, comfort you, but because of what had happened, what had been said, because I thought you must be hating me I did nothing! You walked, ate, dressed yourself, but you were like a robot, a pro-grammed doll!'

'Was I?' she asked worriedly.

'Yes.'

'Oh, but that was from worry, lack of sleep—'

'I know! And it nearly broke my heart!'

'But I'm better now,' she insisted quietly, yet more troubled in some ways than she had been previously. How could she not have known that he was blaming himself for *her*? 'I'm sorry.'

'For what?' he demanded. 'Being human?' His ex-pression softening, he smoothed away her frown, sighed. 'Just what you need, isn't it? A lecture from me of all people.' Gently smoothing the hair he'd so roughly pushed back, he arranged it in a dark fan across her shoulder, continued to stroke it, and moved his eyes back to hers.

'I watched you as you catnapped in the hospital, and I felt so totally inadequate. All my life I've been strong, arrogant, and I watched you like a helpless child.

'You erupted into my life—a hard, tough lady with an expression in your eyes that seemed to damn all men as fools—arrived in my home as though you had the right to be there, a right to castigate me—and I behaved as though I had a moral right to correct, re-prove—and then I kissed you, and it all changed, until

Tom—your Tom,' he added, with a bitterness that shocked her, 'said what he said.'

'He's not *my* Tom,' she denied.

'Isn't he?'

'No.'

'Then why did he come?'

Searching his eyes, she shook her head. 'I don't know. But he isn't my Tom...' Recalling suddenly that Tano had already gone to his room when she and Tom had talked about themselves, she put out a hesitant hand and touched his cheek. 'I don't know why he came. I'd always told him I didn't love him, would not marry him...'

' "Didn't"?'

'No. Would it have—mattered?' she asked carefully.

'Yes.' And then he gave a rueful smile, allowed the tension to seep out of him. 'I was jealous.'

'Jealous?'

'Yes. I had kissed you, held you, wanted more, and suddenly there was Tom—who could also kiss you.'

'But you offered him brandy,' she said stupidly.

'It was either that or...' With a wry grin, he left the sentence unfinished.

'But you're always so controlled!'

'Am I? I'm also Italian.' The smile in his eyes warm, tender, slightly rueful, he framed her face and added huskily, 'So beautiful.'

'Nothing special,' she corrected shakily.

'No. Egyptian princess, Roman empress. A gold circlet here,' he murmured, touching her forehead, 'and here,' touching her throat. 'Elongated eyes, searching, sexy; a beautiful nose, wide mouth for loving—'

'Or arguing.'

He smiled. 'I almost yearn to hear you argue again, to sleep in your arms,' he continued softly, lovingly, 'to wake to your smile. To love, to touch, to feel, enjoy. To laugh—'

'We never did much laughing, did we?' she asked sadly.

'No, but we will, won't we? Don't disturb me any more. I'll end up neurotic—a wreck of a man. Gibbering—'

'Never. Kiss me,' she blurted out.

'Where?' he asked thickly.

'Everywhere.'

He wrenched his shirt over his head, but carefully unbuttoned hers and moved the halves apart, and his skin felt hot, feverish, his muscles hard, rigid, and his hands were shaking, his breathing erratic—as was hers.

He touched his fingers to her midriff, making her shiver, to her ribs, and then he groaned deep in his throat, gathered her more warmly against him, and his long fingers stroked her soothingly as his mouth, a contrast that blew her mind, branded every inch of flesh he could reach without releasing her.

He undressed her with care, as though she were fragile, tossed aside the rest of his clothes, and their breath hissed in unison when their flesh met, cold at first, then warm, soft, almost flowing together as though their bodies had known all along what was in store.

And he made love to her as she had always yearned to be loved—with strength and passion, warmth and tenderness, with a shivering need that left them helpless, aching. And like a trusting child she curled against him and slept.

They remained at the villa for two more days—as lovers. And then reluctantly he informed her that he must return to Rome.

'So many things left unfinished—things I *must* do.'

'I know.' Smiling at him, loving him, she pushed her fingers through his short, springy hair, loving the feel of it—of him. 'You're a very important man.'

'A very busy man,' he corrected. 'I delegated as much as I could whilst Umberto and your mother were seriously ill, delegated even more when I could no longer concentrate without seeing you, but now...'

'The real world beckons?'

'Intrudes.' He smiled. 'Not beckons. You will be able to amuse yourself whilst I work?'

'Yes, of course.' And in her naïvety she thought she could, thought it would be simple.

'I realise that you will need to return to England to put your own affairs to rights, but will you stay for a few days? A week?'

Almost shocked, because in truth she had given very little thought to Tom, Lucy, the animals since they'd been at the villa, she nodded. Did he mean that was *all* he wanted from her? Or did he mean her to settle her affairs and then return to Rome? She didn't know—and didn't know how to ask.

She'd been content to let him have the ordering of her life over the past few days, to dictate what they should do, but now he'd forced her to think about the future and she didn't now know what was expected of her, what she herself wanted.

She loved him, but no commitment had been mentioned. Only then did she remember his words in the catacombs—she was an 'experiment', and he didn't want to be 'disturbed'. Was this just an interlude? And, like Piers, would he one day disappear from her life?

The following morning—the morning they were to return to Rome—lying awake in the wide bed, still troubled by her thoughts of the day before, Rea listened to the sounds of Tano in the shower, then gave a faint smile when she heard his awful singing.

That was one thing he *couldn't* do—unlike love-making, which he *could*, and had been doing on and off for the past few days to perfection. Hours, days of giving, gentle warmth, passion—and now he sounded pleased to be returning to Rome, to his busy life there.

With a long, worried sigh, wishing that she could see into the future, she turned her gaze to the window, watched clouds chase each other across the blue sky— white, insubstantial, *happy* clouds.

She knew what she wanted, but she didn't know if it was possible. Tano was warm and kind, generous, but she didn't know if he loved her, and, even if he did, was it the love she knew she now needed—a love like the one Umberto and her mother had?

When the water stopped running she turned her head and smiled as Tano emerged, a towel round his neck—but not round his hips. 'Naked and unashamed,' she murmured, admiring the length of him, the strength, remembering that other day when she'd seen him wet from his shower and desire had curled in her stomach. Then she'd been too upset to look. Now she could.

'You want me to be ashamed?' he asked softly, with that quirky smile that so delighted her, but there was an eagerness about him now, as though he yearned to be back among familiar things, as though a nice little interlude was—ending?

'No,' she denied. 'I'll go and have my shower.' As she passed him she halted, gave in to compulsion and ran a gentle, almost proprietorial hand down his damp back, shivered with renewed desire as she pressed a kiss to his shoulder. 'You have a lovely body,' she murmured as she allowed her tongue to taste his warm flesh.

'So do you.' Turning, he gathered her close, pressed her length to his, and desire became rampant. Mouths that had so recently clung clung once more. Kissing him, holding him, the feel of his tongue on hers, the way he kissed the *inside* of her lower lip sent her body into shock, slammed overwhelming longing into them both.

One strong hand grasped her thigh, lifted, and she clung, awkwardly balanced on one leg, arched into him, and the groan of need was torn from her. 'Oh, Tano, Tano. Don't be gentle,' she begged. 'Dear God, don't be gentle.'

Tense, hot, his skin burning hers, he stepped back, sat on the edge of the bed, drew her astride him. His mouth open against her neck, arms an unbreakable barrier around her, he held her, rocked slowly back and forth, back and forth. Eyes tight shut, head thrown back, she gave in to the pleasure that swamped her, dug her fingers into his shoulders, brushed her full breasts against his chest, until an explosion of pleasure released them.

Falling backwards, his breathing as ragged as her own, eyes closed, he spread his arms wide in a gesture of supplication.

Drawing her knees up to ease the pressure on their joined bodies, she stared at him, admired him, loved him. He lifted his lashes, and she gave a shaky smile.

'Wow?' she teased, her voice distorted. 'Or oh, my goodness?'

His eyes crinkled, and then he began to smile—a wide, beautiful, blinding smile. His voice soft, throaty, he said something in Italian that she didn't understand, and when she asked him what it meant he shook his head, reached out a gentle hand and removed a stray lock of hair from her cheek. 'Something to savour.'

'Yes.'

'Kiss me,' he ordered softly. 'Then go have your shower.'

Leaning forward, her weight on her arms, she pressed her mouth to his, then got to her feet. 'And you do have nice legs,' she praised as she went into the bathroom and closed the door. But not curls, she thought, remembering those beautiful statues.

'Did someone say otherwise?' he called, sounding comically puzzled.

'No. Only me.'

It couldn't end, could it? Not something like this, something so incredibly special. But it might not be incredibly special to him. Maybe he'd felt like that with all the women he had loved. Her troubled frown returning, she stood beneath the warm water, tilted

her face to the spray as though she might wash away
her thoughts, and when she came out as naked as he,
rubbing absently at her hair, she stood for a while
watching him as he stood at the window and gazed
out over the lake.

What do you want of me? she wanted to ask. But
asking would require an answer, and that was what
she was afraid of—the answer.

They reached Rome at lunchtime, arriving to heat and
humidity and a ringing phone. They both paused, the
memory of illness and accident still too new to be
totally discounted, and then he quickly lifted the receiver—and relaxed. 'Angélique,' he murmured, and
gave Rea a quick smile.

Angélique. Who was Angélique—the woman he'd
been talking to on the steps? The woman he'd sat with
in the back of the car? Beautiful, sophisticated ... a
threat? Tano replaced the receiver, turned to smile at
her and gave a shrug of apology. 'She's coming round.
There are papers that need to be looked at, decisions
to be made.'

'It's all right,' Rea said simply. But it wasn't, and
that was stupid. 'I'll go and unpack.'

He nodded, his mind already on his work.

Angélique was every bit as lovely as Rea remembered.
She was also polite and not exactly unfriendly, but—
superior? Certainly brisk, important, and she spoke
perfect English.

She smiled distantly at Rea, nodded, asked after
her mother and Umberto, even apologised for in-
truding, then went on to explain unnecessarily that

Gaetano was important, that a great deal of work had been neglected. And then she spent a lot of time looking over Tano's shoulder at papers, diagrams, one slim hand resting near his neck, her breath feathering his hair, and jealousy twisted Rea's insides.

Hurrying into the kitchen, Rea made coffee. Then she unpacked, sat and watched television, read a magazine, a book. At eleven she went to bed. She didn't think they even noticed her going.

The next morning Angélique was back with yet more papers. Tano grimaced an apology but that was all, and Rea did not think she could bear to watch those two heads close together for any more hours.

They spoke, naturally, in Italian, which Rea did not understand, and even if she had she would not have understood the content. With much of the same over the next few days, it opened up a gulf between them— a gulf Rea did not know how to bridge.

Tano became impatient, irritable, as did she, and when she found him disrupting the newly tidied lounge she demanded crossly, 'What are you looking for?'

'Papers.'

'What papers? Tano!' she insisted, when he didn't answer but merely continued tossing documents around in the bureau. '*What* papers?'

'An assessment,' he muttered irritably. 'I do wish you wouldn't *move* things!'

'I haven't moved anything!'

'You do not need to clean! I told you that! I will not have you being *domestic*.'

'Well, what else am I supposed to do—trail around after you and Angélique?' And she hadn't meant the woman's name to come out sounding so spiteful, but it had, and she wasn't really surprised when he turned to give her a look of disgust.

Straightening, he said with quiet dignity, 'Angélique is a colleague. That is *all* she is. I have apologised for neglecting you, for my need to be busy. A few more days and then things will, I hope, return to normal. Please, Rea, don't be—peevish!'

'I'm not being peevish,' she muttered. But she was. 'Now where are you going?' she asked awkwardly as he strode to the door.

'Another meeting. I should not be late.'

'What about your papers?'

'I will have to go without them. I'll see you later.'

Yes, she thought drearily. Later.

Ashamed of herself, of her bad temper, she did try to be understanding, loving, but she had too much time on her hands—time when Tano was out in the field or at the institute or some function that decreed dressing up, and so her feelings of inadequacy deepened, as did the jealousy.

She had never been jealous before, had never understood the emotion—until now. Sometimes he didn't come to bed until two or three in the morning—when she feigned sleep—and sometimes they made love, but something now was missing.

On the Friday, one week after they had returned to Rome, he came home early bearing flowers—a huge bouquet which he solemnly presented to her.

'I've neglected you shamefully.'

'Understandable,' she murmured, and was horrified to hear the sulky note in her voice.

'Is it?' he asked gently.

'Yes.' But she kept her face averted because she felt guilty for doubting him, guilty for feeling jealous—and angry for feeling diminished.

'You have rung your mother today? Umberto?'

'Yes.' As she did every day. They had gone to stay at a small convalescent home on the south coast to rest and recover before the painful and lengthy skin grafting began. And it was time for her to go home, she thought sadly.

'They are well?'

'Yes. Fine.'

'Good. You went shopping as I bade you?'

She nodded, still a little puzzled as to why she needed something extra smart. 'Where is it that we're going? A function at the institute?'

'No, to keep a promise I once made.'

'Promise?'

'Mmm. The Hassler?'

'Oh. You don't have to—'

'Yes, Rea, I do. You don't wish to go?'

'Yes, of course.'

'Then you have three hours in which to make yourself beautiful.'

As beautiful as Angélique? she wondered. Forcing a smile, she thanked him for the flowers, stood on tiptoe to kiss him, and found that she wanted to cry.

'Go put your flowers in water; I'm going to shower.'

'Tano?'

He turned, and perhaps her voice was different, or the way she stood, because his smile was gone and he looked wary and that, of all things, made her a coward.

'Nothing,' she murmured, taking the easy way out. 'How posh have I to be?'

He smiled, but it didn't quite reach his eyes. 'Very.'

Feeling unsure, indecisive, knowing they were drifting but uncertain how to make things change, Rea went to arrange her flowers.

When she'd had her own shower she found underwear, suspender belt and stockings—all bought by Tano because he'd longed to see her legs, because she hadn't brought any smart clothes with her and he was sick of seeing her in jeans. Sitting at the dressing-table she began to blow-dry her hair, then twisted the long, shining strands into a complicated knot on top of her head.

When they were both ready they stood side by side before the mirror—a handsome couple. Evening dress looked well on Tano. Well? she thought with inward anguish. He looked devastating.

'Did you know,' she asked softly, 'that you look like Hadrian's lover, Antinous?'

A small smile quirked his mouth. 'But without his proclivities, I hope.'

'Mmm.'

'And you look stunning.'

'Thank you.' As stunning as Angélique? she wondered.

Turning to her, he gently fingered the soft drape of her black dress, traced the narrow red piping at the neck and short sleeves, the large red button off-centre at the waist. 'You have good taste. No, you have *excellent* taste.' He smiled. 'But then you have an excellent shape. Ready?'

'Yes. I'm sorry I was a grouch.'

'You're forgiven.'

But it would be easier, she wanted to tell him, if I knew how you felt about me—how you *really* felt. But now was not the time to ask. Picking up her black clutch bag, she followed him out.

It should have been special—and it was special in a way. It was a beautiful restaurant with wide glass windows overlooking the city, and they stood for a while just staring out at the rooftops, at the overcast sky, at the street below, until taking their places at a small table in the corner.

A red rose stood in the centre of the snowy-white tablecloth; the subdued lighting glinted off the tableware, and she smiled across at him—the handsomest man in town. No, not handsome, she mentally corrected; handsome always conjured up conceit in her mind, and he wasn't—just proud, clever, harshly attractive. Except when he smiled, as he was doing now, and then he was devastating. Sadness fell over her like a cloak, because if things continued as they were she would have to go home. She *knew* she would.

This last week had shown her that sharing his life would be difficult. Living in a foreign city without anything to occupy her would be almost impossible. She would become even more cranky and bad-tempered, more jealous of his work, his colleagues. Already she was beginning to feel useless—not a feeling she had ever been used to. And perhaps he knew; perhaps that was the reason for the meal—a little treat before they said goodbye. Life with him would be possible if he loved her, if some sort of commitment had been made, because then she would know what she had to do—learn the language, find occupation... But not knowing made it difficult to burn bridges. So she had to ask, didn't she? Otherwise—

'What's wrong?' he asked gently.

'Nothing,' she replied, her voice husky, and she quickly cleared her throat. 'I just feel—undeserving.' Forcing another smile, she shook her head as though to deny it, and, thankfully, at that point the waiter presented her with the menu, and for a while she was able to pretend that everything was fine.

They didn't talk very much, just smiled at each other, touched fingers across the table like real lovers, as though they had a future, and she wasn't sure they had. But because he'd gone to so much trouble to please her, because he was being so incredibly kind, she pushed her misgivings aside and managed to eat most of the excellent food and drink two glasses of wine. Yet slowly his mood changed, became quiet, reflective, almost sombre.

Watching her across the table, his coffee-cup pushed to one side, Tano complimented her quietly, 'You look—special. Elegant and special. The most beautiful woman in the room. Let's go home.'

And, despite Rea's misgivings, warmth flooded her body, her face, desire darkened her lovely eyes as he called the waiter over and settled the bill. Seemingly incapable of unassisted movement, she waited until he stood, held her chair for her to rise, then tangled her fingers in the hand he held out to her and walked with him to the lift.

As soon as the doors closed he drew her into his arms, tasted her wine-sweet mouth, touched his fingers to her nape, made her shiver convulsively—just as the doors opened onto the crowded foyer.

With a hopelessly wry smile, ignoring the knowing grins of the people who'd seen, he murmured, 'The next restaurant I take you to will be at the top of a very high building, with a lift that takes a long, long time to descend.'

The next restaurant? Did that sound hopeful? As though they had a future? Or had it merely been something to say? 'First mud wrestlers,' she quipped shakily, 'and now a lift fetish. What else don't I know about you, Tano?'

'A great deal,' he said quietly. Taking her hand again, he led her outside. The rain clouds had all gone, leaving the sky sparkling and clear, dotted with stars. A taxi pulled up and he helped her inside, spoke quickly with the driver.

'What did you say to him?' she asked curiously.

'To take the long route home, and not to look.'

Her voice barely audible, she whispered, 'And what will we be doing that he mustn't look at?'

'This,' he breathed. Narrowing the last little distance between them, he touched his mouth incredibly gently to hers, gathered her close, and began to kiss her with slow seduction.

Her bag fell unheeded to the floor as she slid her arms round his neck, touched her fingers to his thick, short hair. She was almost supernaturally aware of the weave of his jacket—the multitude of threads that made up the collar, the lapel—the softness of his shirt as she slid her hand to cover his heart, unconsciously regulated her breathing to his as their mouths continued to cling, taste, explore with gentle insistence.

Her skirt had ridden up above her knees, exposing her long thighs to the touch of his, and she slipped off a shoe and began to massage his ankle with her toes. He gave a little grunt, moved one hand to a silk-clad thigh, then jumped in shock when a horn blared loudly directly beside them, and their driver wound down his window, shouting something obviously rude.

The mood broken, they looked at each other, grinned, and Rea giggled.

'Forgot where I was for a moment,' Tano chuckled. 'And I've missed you—missed this. An impossible week.' Leaning forward, he tapped the driver on the shoulder, told him to take them home.

Rescuing her shoe and bag, she smoothed her skirt modestly over her knees and gave him a teasing sideways grin, because his words had given her hope, and he laughed. 'Thank goodness I don't have to kiss you goodnight on the doorstep.'

'Don't be too sure,' she warned mockingly. 'I might have a headache.'

'I don't know about a headache, I'm certainly intending you to have—'

Hastily putting her hand over his mouth, she shook her head at him in mock reproach. 'Uh-uh, gentlemen never specify.'

'Who said I was a gentleman?'

'I did. And here we are—home.'

Except it wasn't. Standing on the pavement whilst Tano paid the driver—generously, she was sure—Rea shivered a little in the cool evening air, and her mood changed again. Staring up at the stars, she wondered if praying for guidance would do any good, but she smiled when he joined her, and, with his arm draped companionably round her shoulders, they went up.

Halting her on the dim landing, he drew her into his arms, smiled down into her upturned face. 'I'm going to make love to you,' he told her throatily, 'until you can't think, can't talk, can't breathe. And then I'm going to make love to you again.'

'Are you?' she whispered happily as her body, in anticipation, began to respond.

'Yes. And tomorrow we are going to drive out to the lake, take the telephone off the hook, and spend the whole weekend in bed.'

Desire, want, need warming her bones, she stared into his eyes. 'Sounds good,' she approved faintly.

'Only good?'

'Excellent. Stupendous. Wonderful.'

'But first . . .'

'Yes,' she agreed softly. 'First.' They smiled at each other; he found his key and opened the door—and found Angélique waiting for them.

He looked aggravated, irritated, but not surprised—not surprised that she had been able to get *in*. 'Oh, now what?' he demanded frustratedly.

She broke into a flood of Italian, and it sounded impatient. She *looked* impatient, as though she might have been pacing. She looked at Rea, gave a distant nod, then looked back at Tano, and he nodded, muttered something under his breath, and hurried into the bedroom. Barely acknowledging the other woman, Rea hurried after him. 'What?' she demanded. 'What's happening?'

Busily shedding his clothes, hunting for jeans and a work shirt, he explained quickly, disgustedly, 'Some lunatic has got into one of my tunnels and now he's stuck. Rea, I'm sorry, but I shall have to go, I can't have amateurs digging around ruining things.'

'But surely there's someone else who could go?'

'Apparently not. I should only be a couple of hours.'

'And that's it? Angélique beckons and you run?'

He went very, very still. 'Yes, Rea. Angélique beckons and I run. *Because*,' he added with marked intensity, 'she does not call unless it is urgent—imperative. She is a colleague—a well-respected colleague—who shares my fear of damage. You think I *want* to go?'

'Yes,' she said quietly. 'That's exactly what I think.'

He looked at her long and hard, walked across, touched his fingers to her cheek, and she shrugged petulantly away—and then it was too late to wish she hadn't, because his face changed, became hard. Turning away, he wrenched his shirt off a hanger and shrugged into it.

Her hand out in silent apology—an apology he didn't see—she slumped down on the edge of the bed, and her words seemed to form all by themselves. 'I might as well go home, mightn't I?'

He swore, sounding savage and, momentarily abandoning the transfer of his belongings from his dinner suit, he said, 'I expected better of you—not this overreaction. You know you are being stupid.'

'Is that what I'm being—stupid?'

'Yes. And like most women you throw something into the pot in the hope of it being denied. A dangerous game, Rea.'

'Is it? And you know a lot about women, don't you, Tano?'

'Yes. Have known, do know, and right at this moment I'm beginning to wonder why I wanted to know you. Did you expect me to drop important work just to be with you? Expect me to abandon my career, the work I love, just because you're bored and frustrated? Because I can *afford* to? It doesn't work like that, Rea. I'm Italian, not like your milksop Englishmen, content to be ruled by their women.'

'That's not fair.'

'Isn't it? Don't you rule Tom?'

'No.'

'No—you just want the ordering of your own days. As I do. And this talk is long overdue, isn't it? But not now. Now I don't have time.'

'As you never have time.'

He dipped his head in arctic agreement, and continued transferring his belongings.

And now she'd made him angry, prodded when she should have understood—even if the understanding was a pretence—but, on her own road to hell, she couldn't seem to stop. 'Was it just an interlude, Tano?' she asked quietly.

'What?'

'Because, you see, I don't know what you want of me, don't know how I'm supposed to behave—and I'm having a little trouble competing with Angélique and her demands.'

'It is not a competition.'

'Isn't it?'

'No, and if you think it is then I think you have some serious thinking to do.'

'Yes. So I'd best go home, hadn't I?'

Hoping, praying, *expecting*, after what he'd said in the taxi, that he would try to change her mind, would argue, or at least ask her when she would be back, his simple affirmative threw her.

'Yes.' Snapping up his keys, he walked out.

Oh, Tano.

Had someone else once suggested he give up his work, devote his time to her? It wasn't what she wanted. None of this was what she wanted. And she'd been behaving like a spoilt child, hadn't she? Handling everything all wrong. But she'd been afraid of losing him—as she had once lost Piers. And had now promoted the very thing she'd been afraid of.

She heard the front door close with a muted bang, and didn't know what to do, didn't know how to call him back with Angélique within earshot. What did you expect, Rea? she asked herself. That he would declare his undying love for you? No, she hadn't expected that, but then, she hadn't meant to say what she'd said either. She should have commiserated with him, sympathised... If she'd been a nice person she would have.

Why can't you learn to keep your tongue between your teeth, Rea? She would apologise when he came back. Be kind, loving... Perhaps then he would say all the things she yearned for him to say.

And how had she come to this? she wondered despairingly. She should be either packing and going home or out there fighting for his love, not behaving like a wet rag. Tossing her bag onto the dressing-table, she got ready for bed.

And she needed to know now, didn't she, how he really felt? And so she must ask him. When he came back they must sit down, talk. Plans could be made—if he wanted her. She would learn Italian, maybe learn about archaeology—but perhaps he didn't want her to learn. That was the trouble; she didn't know *what* he wanted, and, perhaps because of Piers, had never asked.

She'd asked Piers and he'd looked surprised, as though she should have known. And then she'd begged—and he'd looked horrified. Is that how Tano would look?

She had thought herself confident, in control; she would always ask when she didn't know the answer to something—often aggressively—but now she couldn't, in case the answer wasn't one she wanted to hear. And if she did ask and he said no, what then? Then you get on with your life, Rea, and stop being a fool!

She dozed fitfully, afraid to sleep in case she missed hearing him come in, and then, just before eight, she heard Tano's key in the lock of the front door. Shrugging into her dressing-gown, relieved, knowing what she must say, she hurried to meet him—and found Angélique. Even in cotton trousers and shirt she looked elegant.

Feeling at a distinct disadvantage, Rea tightened the belt on her robe and waited.

Angélique smiled. 'Gaetano has asked me to come to explain that he will be about two hours more. You understand?'

'Yes, of course,' Rea agreed, not sure that she did. Had he sent a message because he was worried that she might worry? Or to prevent another argument? 'Can I get you a coffee or something?'

'Coffee would be nice. We can then perhaps talk whilst we have it.'

That sounded ominous. Talk about what? Or had Angélique meant nothing? Was it just her way of saying 'gossip', much as her mother did over the fence? Only, somehow Angélique didn't look the sort of woman to chat over a garden fence. Leading the way into the kitchen, Rea put the coffee on to boil, indicated for the other woman to sit.

'Gaetano is much admired,' Angélique began. 'Revered.'

'Yes,' Rea agreed inadequately.

'Very busy.'

'Yes.'

'Important.'

'Yes.'

'I do not wish to speak out of turn—'

'Don't you?' Rea asked quietly as she faced the other woman. 'What is it you want to say, Angélique?'

'Oh, just clarification, I think. You do not like me, do you?'

'I barely know you,' Rea evaded.

'No. Is difficult, isn't it? You cannot share his work, his language—'

'Not at the moment,' Rea put in. Don't lose your temper, she cautioned herself. Listen to what Angélique has to say—and then lose your temper. 'You think I'm unsuitable for him? Is that it?'

'Not unsuitable, no,' Angélique denied, not one whit discomposed by Rea's blunt speaking. 'It is not my place to say who is suitable or unsuitable... You have had much anguish—your parents—and Gaetano too has been worried, but—'

'But you think I've been here long enough.'

With a little shrug and a rather wry smile, Angélique nodded. '*Sì*. He has so much work he has neglected; he is a very busy man, with no time to study things as he ought. This newly formed commission is taking up too much time, and until he is able to find competent people to delegate to...

'You understand what I am saying? Gaetano is very much a man, with a man's needs—this I know—but... I do not know how to say this without causing offence. There have been many women in Gaetano's life, but only for—short times. Loredana is for little while, then Claudia, and now you. But...'

'But Gaetano does not want commitment?'

'*Sì*,' she agreed in relief.

'And I'm a distraction he doesn't need?'

'He is so *busy*. And last night you have made him angry...' With a deep sigh Angélique continued, 'It is not for myself that I want him; I too do not wish for commitment. I would not like you to think I am jealous woman, but...'

If she said 'but' once more Rea thought she would become violent, and was Angélique saying that she and Tano had been lovers? Would be lovers again? Because neither of them wanted commitment, only— sexual release? 'Don't you think it is for Gaetano to tell me to go?'

'Yes, but he will not, because of your upset over your parents, because you have been hurting, because he was arbitrary—is this right?—over the land.'

'He told you about that?'

'Of course. We are colleagues.'

Yes, colleagues—as she could never be. And Angélique was interfering for Gaetano's good, not out of spite or a malicious desire to wound, or even out of jealousy, but because she was a colleague and Gaetano was too busy for—distraction. 'Gaetano asked you to speak to me?' she asked, with a blandness Tano might have been proud of.

'Of course not.'

'I'm very glad to hear it. Then, when I go—*if* I go—I'm sure you will be the very first to know of it.'

Angélique gave a theatrical little sigh, as though dealing with a fractious child. 'It is not my wish to hurt you, merely to protect Gaetano. Already there has been talk at the institute—unsavoury jokes that I do not wish to come to his ears.' Hesitating a moment, she added, 'You do understand that he *is* very important? That he is not—ordinary? That his family are influential?'

'Yes.' And that was definitely a warning. Was the class system in Italy worse than the class system that had existed in the last century at home? Was it not desirable for an ordinary English girl to mix in such circles? And, despite the friendship and kindness she had received, that was part of the trouble—Rea did not *know*.

Had she inadvertently upset someone when refusing Umberto's numerous invitations for her to meet people? Was that partly why her mother had been so upset? But, even if it was, it wasn't Angélique's place to tell her so. And just how much of the other woman's words was truth, how much speculation?

Suddenly, Rea longed for the familiarity of her own home, people she understood, a *language* she understood.

'If you love him, as I think, perhaps, you do, then do you not wish the best for him?'

'Your best? Or his?' Rea asked quietly.

'Perhaps a little of both,' Angélique admitted honestly. 'After all, I'm the one who has the heavy workload when he is otherwise—engaged.' Getting to her feet, she added, 'I will not, I think, wait for coffee.' With a dignity that Rea envied, she let herself out.

Because Gaetano was longer than the two hours promised by Angélique Rea had too much time to mull over their conversation, too much time to get angry about it, and so when the doorbell rang and she found a rather voluptuous female on her doorstep she was in no mood to be polite. Neither was the other woman, judging by her manner.

'Yes?' Rea demanded frostily.

'Gaetano?'

'No. He isn't here.'

'I wait.' Pushing past Rea, she stalked into the lounge just as Tano appeared on the landing. And Rea was in no mood to notice his tiredness, only his irritability.

'Was that Claudia?' he demanded.

'How would I know?'

With a muttered imprecation, he walked past her. A flood of Italian followed. Both sounded angry, but then, Italians having a normal conversation always sounded angry to Rea.

Slamming the front door shut, she stormed into the lounge. 'Excuse me,' she interrupted icily. 'I appreciate that my wishes are not likely to count, but in *England*,' she berated forcefully, 'one does not enter another person's home without an invitation! And, although this might only be my *temporary* home, that *is* what it *is*!'

Turning on Tano, she continued furiously, 'And I would be enormously grateful if you would not discuss my private affairs with all and sundry! How dare you tell Angélique about my affairs? It has nothing to do with her! And don't send her as your messenger! In future use the damned phone!'

Before he could speak, answer, defend himself—if indeed he had been going to—she continued wrathfully, 'And there was no need to be shy about telling me to go after my *trauma*!' she spat out. 'All you had to do was *say*!'

And Tano just stood there. Waited. His face closed. And when she said nothing further he asked quietly, 'You're packed?'

'Packed?' she asked blankly.

'*Sì*. Packed.'

Shocked, she just stared at him. He wanted her to go? Now? No discussion? No—anything? 'No!'

Deliberately misunderstanding, he offered, 'Then I suggest you do so. Now. I'll run you to the airport.'

Choked, disbelieving, a hard pain in her chest, she whispered bleakly, 'There's nothing I need to take.'

'In that case—'

'What did Angélique say? Because she's obviously said something.'

'A few home truths. Ready?'

'And if I'm not? Don't want to go?' she asked pleadingly.

'Don't play games,' he ordered, suddenly savage. 'Do not, please, play games.'

Grasping Claudia's arm, he shoved her out ahead of him, then gave Rea a long, hard look and waited for her to leave too. His face held an expression of carved distaste.

Picking up her handbag, which held her passport and credit cards, Rea moved numbly after Claudia. Too late now to explain that her outburst had been caused by fear because she'd been unsure of herself. And even if it hadn't been too late she didn't think she'd have been able to say anything without crying, pleading, begging his forgiveness.

Claudia stalked off along the pavement, head held high, back quivering. With indignation?

Rea got into the car.

CHAPTER SEVEN

THIS was wrong, Rea thought, saying goodbye to Tano in a busy airport. There was no privacy, no way to say all the things she wanted to say—things he no longer wanted her to say. Certainly he didn't give the impression of a man awaiting explanation. He looked like a man who'd made up his mind—a man who'd had more than enough.

There was no direct flight available, but there was one via Paris. Tano bought her ticket, then checked her case in, lifted it onto the ramp, made sure she had all her papers—all in silence—then escorted her to the barrier.

Frightened, wanting to beg, she turned, grasped his arm, and he stared down at her, his face stern.

'Thank you for all you've done,' she began, her voice low, uneven.

'Don't,' he gritted, 'thank me!' His mouth a grim line, he suddenly pulled her against him, and, as though to imprint his mark upon her for all time, kissed her hard. Then he released her and walked away. He didn't look back.

Tears blurring her vision, Rea watched his tall figure until he was out of sight. It felt as though she would never see him again. Perhaps she wouldn't. Quickly showing her passport, she hurried through the barrier. There was a raw, hard lump in her chest.

* * *

It was early evening when she got home. She went straight to Tom's practice—and discovered something that she should have discovered a long time ago. Lucy and Tom were there together—and she suddenly knew why Tom had come out to Rome.

They swung round, stared at her, and both looked—guilty.

'You came to Rome to tell me that you'd fallen in love with Lucy, didn't you?'

He looked relieved, nodded. 'Yes. I thought it only fair to tell you—tell you at once.' He gave a brief, unamused laugh. 'I had it all planned, and then I couldn't find you, got soaking wet, angry—no, furious—so that when I did find you, discovered you with *him*—a man who always makes other men feel inferior, inadequate—'

'Does he?' Rea asked in astonishment.

'Yes. And so I lost my temper. I'm sorry.'

'No, I'm the one to be sorry. I drew you both into this mess . . .' Glancing at Lucy—gentle, hardworking Lucy—she forced a smile. 'Now I understand why you sounded so evasive.'

'Yes,' Lucy mumbled awkwardly. 'I felt so guilty. We didn't mean it to happen; it just did. I've always liked Tom but I thought he loved you, and then when you were away we got on so well, and I thought . . .'

'That if he spoke to me it would all be spoilt.'

'Yes.'

And that was why she hadn't told him the new number.

'And then . . .' Tom tailed off with a wry shrug. Glancing at Lucy, he smiled warmly, hugged her to his side, and Rea felt jealous of their closeness, their love when she had just lost hers. Tom's look said it all—said that they had made love, and that the time for pretending was over. 'And then I came out. I made rather a fool of myself, didn't I?'

'No. I did.'

'You love him, don't you? Your Italian friend?'

'Yes.' No point in denying it, even to herself.

'So you'll be going back to Italy. You won't need to worry about the wildlife; we'll look after them—without payment,' he added. 'Sorry about that; did he tell you?'

Rea nodded.

'Want me to sell your camper? I can put the money in your account, get it transferred to Italy.'

He was so eager to have it all cleared up. She wanted to tell him not to rush her, but she held back, bit her lip. They wanted her out of their lives, wanted to be settled, and Rea could understand that, could understand that Lucy wouldn't want her around—a constant reminder that Tom had once thought himself in love with her—any more than she had wanted Claudia around.

Because that had been the last straw, to see the sort of woman Tano had been attracted to—warm, sensual, voluptuous. Not a sharp-tongued, shrewish English girl.

Tom glanced at his watch and grimaced. 'Rounds to do, I'm afraid.' He released Lucy, held out his hand for Rea to shake, and with a helpless little grunt of laughter that verged on tears she did so and wished him well. And when he'd gone she faced Lucy—a rather defiant Lucy.

'I'm thirty-three,' Lucy stated quietly, 'and you never really wanted him, did you?'

'No.'

'I didn't mean to go behind your back...'

'I know.'

'You don't mind?'

Rea shook her head.

'You're going back to Italy?'

'Yes.' And she knew that she would. Tano probably would not want her back, but if by some remote chance he did then even a minute of his time had to be worth a lifetime without him. And if he did not want her then she would have to come to terms with it in her own way.

Hiding had never solved anything. Running away had never solved anything. And she loved him. Sitting on the plane, even tired and hurting, she had had too much time to think—time to *know* how much she loved him. Anyway, she'd have to be in Italy for her mother's skin grafts. Wanted to be there. *Needed* to be there. She had almost lost her once...

'You should have *told* me the animals weren't supposed to be on that land,' Lucy reproved her.

'I know.' With a deep sigh of her own, feeling just as helpless as Lucy looked, Rea gave an odd little smile.

'I'm sorry about your parents.'

'Thank you.'

'Are they all right?'

'Yes.'

'I'd have fought for him, you know. If you'd come back and said you wanted him I'd have fought for him.'

'Yes.' And if Lucy—gentle, inoffensive Lucy—could fight for Tom, why in the name of all that was wonderful couldn't she have fought for Tano? Rationally, without resorting to childish tantrums? Why, in fact, had she allowed Angélique to do his talking for him?

Had she really believed that Tano didn't have the courage to tell her himself? What sort of woolly thinking had that been? Tano was perfectly capable of terminating his own relationships. He hadn't actually *said* he didn't want her back. They would have been at the lake by now— 'What?'

'I said did you want to check on the animals before you leave?'

'Oh, yes, right.'

Her smile sadly wry, because she was obviously expected to go now, not linger, Rea walked across to the cages lined up against the wall behind the surgery. They looked fine, healthy, except for the baby fox. 'He's not going to make it, is he?' Rea asked sadly.

'No. It would be kinder to have him put down.'

'Yes.' Staring at the ragged little animal, eyes dulled with pain and bewilderment, she bit her lip, nodded. They didn't want her here, didn't *need* her here, and she knew that she needed to be needed, needed to be loved. By Tano.

'Is the camper still on Tano's land?'

'Yes. We didn't know where else to put it.'

'No. OK, I'll go and sort my stuff out, and drop the keys off when I'm ready to leave. If you and Tom will sell it for me...'

'We will. I love you dearly, Rea,' Lucy blurted out. 'But...'

'I know.' And she did. Giving the other woman an impulsive hug, Rea wished her happy, thanked her for all she'd done, and hurried away.

'Rea?' Lucy called. 'Will you keep in touch? Let me know how you are? I didn't mean to be ... I was just ...'

'I know. I hope everything works out for you.'

'I think it will.'

'Yes. I think so too.'

'Shall I run you back to your camper?'

'No, it's not far. The walk will do me good.'

It was odd, Rea thought as she walked; she'd lived here most of her life and now it seemed—unfamiliar, as though she no longer belonged. A past place, no longer the present. It also seemed very English. She had never noticed before how very *green* England was—never consciously noticed, had just taken it for granted.

And, as one day slipped into two, then three, a week, she noticed other things, made comparisons. She missed the warmth, the laughter, the arm-waving, the *energy* of Italy. Without noticing, without thinking about it, she had changed. Become a different person.

And every minute of every day she missed Tano—the scent of him, the taste, the warmth. And she wanted to be held. So why was she wasting time? Because she was afraid to go back? Afraid of the outcome? That was no good. Just do it, Rea, she told herself.

And when she was done, with everything packed, she stared round her, stared at what had been her home for so long. All my worldly goods, she thought wryly, in two suitcases. But there was nothing else she wanted, needed.

After locking up, she carried her cases along to the practice, handed her keys to Lucy, along with her paying-in book so that the money from the sale of the camper could be paid into her account, used the phone to call a cab, kissed Lucy goodbye and wished her luck.

'You won't be back?'

'No.' Even if Tano no longer wanted her she wouldn't be back. It was time to move on—had been time a long while ago. Perhaps she'd finally grown up. There were animals in Italy, veterinary practices, stray cats, probably even foxes. There were certainly birds. Perhaps Umberto would help, or one of his numerous relations. And once she'd learned the language . . .

Eight hours later, her suitcases resting at her feet, Rea was ringing the bell of Tano's apartment. Ten in the evening was probably not the best time to go visiting, but... Nerves twisting in her stomach, hands clammy, she waited.

The door opened, and there he was, tall and beautiful, grey eyes steady. He didn't look shocked, or surprised, just a careful study in neutrality. His index finger held the place in the book he'd obviously been reading, his grey sweatshirt was rumpled, the sleeves pushed up, and old jeans clung lovingly to his long legs. His feet were bare. Never had he looked so inexpressibly dear. And she loved him so much that it cramped her insides, made it impossible to speak.

Tano gazed at her, searched her face. 'Are you staying?' he asked in a pronounced drawl.

'If that's what you want,' she managed quietly.

'If that's what I want? When I've just spent the most miserable week of my entire life?' he asked almost conversationally. Without seeming urgency he dropped the book, pulled her inside, and closed the door.

Five minutes later he opened it, retrieved her suitcases, and closed it again. Dumping them on the floor, he grasped her wrists, put her arms round his neck, and pulled her back into his arms, tight—so tight that she could barely breathe—and she gave a sigh that sounded absurdly blissful. He didn't smile.

'Stand on your toes,' he ordered gruffly.

She stood on her toes.

'Mouth.'

Eyes closed, Rea blindly raised her mouth to his, clutched him as though afraid of falling as he fitted his frame snugly to hers and began to kiss her again with hunger, passion, an almost desperate need.

'You took your time,' he growled softly.

'You knew I'd be back,' she managed, her voice, her whole body shaken.

'Did I?'

'Yes.' Unsure for a moment, she leaned away to look at him. 'Didn't you?'

'No.' Pulling her back against him, refusing her any leeway, he added almost carefully, 'All better?'

'Yes. I saw Lucy.'

He blinked. 'The connection eludes me,' he drawled mockingly.

'I think she'll marry Tom.'

He smiled. 'Good. Soon, I hope.'

'Yes.'

His smile widened, became wry as tension slowly lessened. 'I ought to hate you.'

'Because I ran away?'

'Yes.'

'Do you?'

'No.'

'You made it hard for me to stay.'

'I know.'

'You don't mind being chased?'

'No. *This* time I wanted to be caught.'

'Good. Let's go to bed.'

'How utterly shameless.'

'Yes, but I don't want to waste any more time. You did *want* me to come back?'

'I wanted. Can't you tell?'

Rea smiled, then grinned and gave a little choke of laughter. 'I'm sorry.'

'So you should be.'

'What would you have done if I hadn't come?' she asked with a curious wistfulness.

'Nothing. Why should I?'

'Tano!'

And he grinned—a grin that she wondered if she would ever get used to.

'What would you have done?'

'Oh,' he drawled, 'come to look at the land you appropriated, strode aloofly round the acreage, checked the barn for damage. I'd probably have found something that I could charge you with— malicious damage, that sort of thing.'

'And then?'

'Dragged you back. By your glorious hair.'

'When?'

'Tomorrow, because the longer you stayed away, the less the chances were of you ever coming back.'

'The longer I stayed away,' she said quietly, 'the worse it got. But I didn't know what you wanted, and if you wanted what I prayed you wanted you deserved better.'

'I would have accepted anything I could get.'

'Would you?'

'Yes. Don't you know that?'

'No.'

'And if someone had told me a few weeks ago that I would be making a fool of myself over a woman I would have laughed. A few weeks ago I was a confirmed bachelor; I assumed I would always be a bachelor.'

'Because women upset the tranquillity of your days?' she asked gently.

He gave a rueful smile. 'What a fatuous thing to have said. True,' he added, with a little grin, 'but fatuous.'

'And now you don't want to be a bachelor?' she asked carefully.

'No.'

'You want a mistress?'

'No. Right at this moment I want a lover.'

'To "experiment" with?' she asked quietly, then waited, breath held, for his answer.

'Exper...? Oh.' As recognition dawned Tano had the grace to look sheepish. 'It was then,' he confessed honestly, 'a nice little interlude—or so I thought.'

'And now?'

'Now it isn't.' Taking her hand, he tugged her towards his bedroom, then scooped her up into his arms, hugged her tight, and lay with her on the wide bed. 'Everything changed after the accident—my feelings, my conceptions...'

'So did mine. Tano...' Not quite sure how to ask, she traced imaginary patterns on his sweatshirt. 'Is social standing so very important in Italy? Will my being here hurt your reputation?'

He searched her face, then asked carefully, 'Is that why you left? Because of my reputation?'

'I didn't want to leave at all!' she exclaimed in remembered anguish.

'A bluff that did not work?'

'Yes. No. Oh, I don't know. I was angry, confused, hadn't had any sleep—and Claudia appearing was the last straw,' she muttered shamefacedly. 'And I couldn't think how you could want me after—her,' she mumbled.

'You don't need to say her name with such hatred,' he murmured, trying hard not to smile. 'And if you expect me to denigrate her just to make you happy I won't.'

'No!' she exclaimed. 'No, of course I don't expect that; I just... And it wasn't only that. Angélique said you were important. And I did know that, but...'

'But because I was so busy that last week your confidence took a severe pasting. You think I didn't know how left out you felt? It's not always like that—so frantic. There were so many things to catch up on, and I was frantically trying to find people to delegate to, to give myself more time with you, and just as I was beginning to see the light at the end of the tunnel you began issuing ultimatums.'

'No. Anyway, I had to check on the animals and Lucy,' she mumbled.

'Don't lie to me,' he ordered gently. 'Had that been the case you would have said. I've never known you less than honest—aggressively so.'

'Except once.'

'Except once,' he agreed. 'I knew you were miserable, unhappy; how could I not? And having to rush off just as I was about to explain and really talk to you didn't help, but I expected that when I returned there would still be time.'

'Only I opened my stupid mouth, accused ... You shouldn't have to apologise for your work. I should have understood ... I *did* understand,' she corrected frowningly, 'but emotions make such a muddle of common sense, don't they?'

'Mmm,' he agreed.

Ignoring his amusement, Rea asked bluntly, 'Were you and Angélique ever lovers?'

'No.'

'But other women wanted you to give up your career?'

He nodded.

'Claudia?'

'Loredana. I shouldn't have accused you of that. I knew it wasn't true but I was a man fighting unfamiliar feelings, fighting a commitment I had never wanted. And there was such a look of mutiny on your face.'

'Not mutiny. Pain. Indecision. And you didn't answer me about your reputation.'

'Oh,' he drawled, 'I think I can stand dragging round a funny little English girl.' And, his smile gentle, he added softly, 'I've had the most terrible withdrawal symptoms.'

'So have I.'

Desire darkened his eyes, and then it was as it should be—as it always should have been. He undressed her gently, teased her thickly about wearing a skirt. 'For me?'

'For you,' she confirmed, her voice even huskier.

'Nice legs.'

'Thank you.'

He smiled, lazily trailed a finger between her full breasts, but his hand was shaking, and the laziness was a lie. Meeting her eyes, he groaned, pulled her against him. 'Cool is gone. Blasé is gone; just, please, for pity's sake, love me!'

Pushing Tano onto his back, she rolled to cover him, began to kiss him with feverish haste, and, his urgency as great as hers, the preliminaries were swift. They needed only to love in passion and need, to quench the fire that burned so brightly in them both. And later, when the need was less urgent, there was a quiet, gentle exchange—a soft culmination after all the frustration and hurt, the desire of two people to make amends.

Lying in his arms, content for the first time in weeks, her face warm against his shoulder, Rea's body decided to try and make up for all those sleepless nights. Tiredness stole over her, weighted her lids, and for a while she slept.

*   *   *

The moon shining onto her face woke Rea, and, disorientated for a moment, she turned her head, found Tano leaning up on one elbow, watching her. When he saw that she was awake he smiled, reached out to trail his fingers over her face, then picked up a thick strand of hair and began winding it into a spiral. 'I like to watch you sleep,' he said softly. 'Need to make sure you're still here.'

'I'll always be here—if you want.'

'I want.'

Searching his eyes, she reached up to touch him, let her hand linger on his jaw, his neck, his shoulder, and gave a soft sigh of pleasure. 'I never liked you, you know.'

He gave a grunt of laughter. 'I know.'

'Never wanted to feel like this.'

'Neither did I.'

'You didn't!' she protested.

'Did.'

'Liar.' With an appealing little grin, she confessed, 'I fancied you rotten.'

'I knew.'

'No, you didn't! Did you?'

'Mmm.'

'How embarrassing,' she gurgled. 'No wonder you were so—' Suddenly recalling something he'd once said, she asked, 'You remember when you mentioned that Mum was widowed when I was three?'

'Mmm, vaguely.'

'Well, why did you say, "That accounts for it"?'

He laughed. 'It was your aggression—your complete and utter conviction that you were always right. I decided it was because you'd been spoilt, with no man's hand on the reins to tug you into proper behaviour.'

'Chauvinist! I know I'm a bit forceful—'

'Aggressive,' he put in helpfully.

'All right, aggressive. I don't mean to be,' she murmured. 'I just get impatient . . .'

'When things don't happen fast enough for your liking?'

'I suppose so. Mum said—'

'Shh,' he reproved her gently, 'no post-mortems. This is the new improved Rea . . . Not that I didn't like the old one . . .'

Turning her face up to his, she gave him a look of humorous reproof. 'You didn't like me at *all*.'

'No,' he agreed. 'I was attracted to you, but no, I didn't like you—although I began to change my mind when you walked into the dining-room in your nightie. With your back to the light, I could see every exquisite inch of you—and my concentration fled. Desire reared its ugly head, and I stared at my book—nonchalant to the last—even turned a page, as I recall, and saw not a word of it.'

'I would never have known,' she commented softly. 'But then I never know what you're thinking, feeling. And I don't know if you want me to say this,' she added in a little rush, 'but I have a need to say it.'

She felt his sudden stillness, the way he held his breath for a moment, and clenched her hand on his shoulder to give herself courage. '*Want* to say it, because otherwise—' Breaking off, knowing that there was no way to say it except to say it, she said clearly, 'I love you.' And his breath shuddered out on a long sigh. 'I've loved you for a long time, I think. At the villa, here...'

'Then why did you leave?'

'Because I thought you wanted me to go. When we were at the villa you said you wanted me to stay a week in Rome before I went home to sort out my affairs. And I thought...' And Angélique had said... 'And even if there'd been a chance that you might come to love me... Oh, Tano, I don't know. I just felt so—useless! And Angélique was so beautiful, so competent...'

'But I didn't want Angélique.'

'Didn't you?' she asked quietly, her eyes not quite meeting his. 'Then why did you let me go? When I hesitantly suggested I would stay you told me not to play games. And that hurt, too. So very much. I just didn't know what you wanted.'

'I didn't know myself,' he confessed. 'At the villa I thought I knew, but then...'

'I started getting picky.' Trying for humour that didn't quite come off, Rea added, 'And you thought, Oh, my God, if this is how she's going to be...'

'Something like that.' He smiled. 'Until the Hassler, and the feel of you in the taxi, the *wanting* of you. For all my experience I have never felt as I feel with you. But to ask you to uproot yourself from your country, your friends, when I didn't really know how permanent I wanted it to be... And then I discovered that wanting didn't come into it. *Choice* didn't come into it.'

'I wasn't asking because... I mean, I don't expect it to automatically follow that just because *I*... Stop it!' she reproved him. 'Stop looking at me in that

comically bewildered way. You *know* what I mean! *I*
needed to say it, needed the—honesty.'

'And you need me to be as honest.'

'But not if you don't...'

'Love you?'

'Yes. I'm not asking for anything you aren't prepared to give.'

'That sounds either very brave or very foolish—a
breeding ground for pain and resentment. And if I
can't give what you want, what then?'

'I don't know,' she replied, still carefully avoiding
his eyes. 'I can't ask you to love me if you don't, can
I? I can't change what you are, any more than you
can change me; I just wanted to tell you how I felt.'

'That you love me.'

'Yes.' Piers had laughed when she'd told him, and
Rea prayed fervently—oh, so very hard—that Tano
wouldn't do the same.

He rested his forehead against hers, touched his
mouth to the bridge of her nose. A breath dragged
deep into his lungs; he lifted his head slightly, looked
down into her eyes.

'Don't look so frightened,' he reprimanded her
quietly. 'I discovered a little while ago that I didn't
want to be like Umberto—to spend most of my life
waiting. I want to see my daughter growing up, not
have her fully grown. I did not know I loved you until
a few days after Umberto and your mother had their
accident.'

'You love me?' she put in quickly.

'Yes, of course I do; why else are we here?' he asked
gently. 'But I didn't know if I wanted it to last.
Couldn't envision it being for ever.

'I knew things weren't right between us, knew something was missing. You won't believe how many excuses I trotted out to myself—that you probably knew how I felt but didn't feel the same, that you wanted to leave because you did not love me, *could* not love me. I think I even convinced myself of that— that your petulance, your anger were because you felt trapped in a relationship you didn't want. And it hurt.

'And this last week, moving around in an empty apartment too large for just one person, with too much space where echoes can gather—echoes of you— I thought I would go mad. I would come to England for you, I decided; I would beg. I would shout at you, shake you, force you. I did not know that just one person—one very special person—could take away your reason for living.

'Seeing your mother and Umberto together amused me. I thought it silly and endearing, but really rather odd. I loved them both, but I did not understand their—foolishness. Then. Perhaps because I had never seen my parents like that—as you know, my parents are both dead, I have no brothers or sisters, and apart from all those numerous cousins Umberto and your mother are the nearest I have to family.

'I did not think I *wanted* closeness, didn't think I wanted sharing. But I do. Will you marry me, Rea?'

'Yes.' Dazed, almost uncomprehending, she was barely aware that she'd answered.

'Yes?' he queried, with a funny smile. 'Just like that?'

'Yes.'

'You'd willingly put up with my abstraction, my selfishness? My—rocks?'

'Yes. Who cleaned the apartment before my mother came?'

'What? Good Lord, woman, don't you ever stick to the point?'

'No.' With a little grin, she hugged him, rubbed her nose across his mouth. 'Who? And if you say Claudia you're dead.'

He laughed. 'All washing is sent out and comes back ironed. A delightful and very middle-aged, happily married lady named Maria discreetly enters, puts it all away, washes up, cleans, etcetera, etcetera.'

'She didn't come the week I was here.'

'No, because I hadn't got around to telling her that I needed her again.'

'Oh. Does she like children?'

'*Yes*! Do *you*?'

'I don't know,' she confessed. 'I'm still trying to come to terms with the fact that you love me. That it's all right.'

'Why did you look frightened?'

Ducking her head, Rea trailed her finger down his chest, then sighed. 'Piers.'

'Who is . . .?'

'Was. A man I thought I was in love with when I was eighteen.'

'And?'

'He laughed. When I told him I loved him he laughed. And when I persisted he looked horrified.' Glancing up, she gave her funny little smile. 'I was heartbroken.'

'And I'm like him, aren't I?'

'A bit.'

'And so you never told me how you felt in case I laughed?'

'Maybe.'

'And Piers is the reason you disliked me when we first met?'

'Mmm.'

'I'm not like Piers. And I have *never* laughed at a woman's feelings.'

'No, but I was afraid to... And you did say "experiment".'

'So I did.'

Looking up, she grimaced. 'Are you cross?'

'No.'

'But you have to admit it's been an odd courtship—if courtship it can be called.'

'It can be called whatever you like. And neither of us is a teenager; neither of us is—inexperienced.'

'I'm not *very* experienced,' she protested, just in case he should think—

'I don't want details,' he interrupted quickly. 'Not *ever!*'

'No.' Somewhat startled by his vehemence, she looked at him, then hugged him. 'No. Not that I was intending to—any more than I want to hear about yours.'

'Snake-wielding or otherwise?' He grinned.

'Mmm.' And she *had* to ask. *Had* to because it wouldn't go out of her mind. 'What did she want?' Rea asked hesitantly. 'Claudia?'

'Just to talk,' he said quietly. 'It isn't important. Children?' he prompted.

And if it wasn't important to him then it mustn't be important to her. 'Do you want them?'

'Yes, I rather think I do.'

Snuggling against him, her bare legs entwined with his, revelling in the sheer *comfort* of his warmth, she teased, 'You have a very silly smile on your face.'

Tano gave an embarrassed laugh that was enormously endearing. 'I think I've just become very Italian, wanting a large family. Do *you*?'

Did she? She'd never really thought about it, or not since she'd been in her teens, when all young girls imagined their knight on his white charger and tiny babies to love, but she could picture it now, she found—a sturdy little baby, a boy that would grow up to look like Tano. 'Yes,' she said softly. 'For you.'

'And you will like to live in Rome?'

'Where else would I live now?' Rea asked gently. 'I have no ties to England. Mum and Umberto are here . . .'

'Yes.' Gently smoothing her hair, as though the long strands held an endless fascination for him, he asked, 'What will you do to fill your days? Wildlife in Rome is a little thin on the ground.'

'I don't know. I expect I'll think of something.'

'I'm not—the easiest person to live with,' he confessed, as though she might not somehow know, and she hid a smile. 'I sometimes have to dash off at the crack of dawn... Well, you know that. And I'm often late home, forget meals . . .'

'Now that I know you love me I promise not to chase you around, give you grief, nag,' she commented drily. 'And I doubt if I'll be a conventional sort of wife anyway. Domestic things bore me. Italian matron I'm not—nor ever will be, I think. I might *try*, but I feel I should warn you that I'll very likely fail. For one thing I can't cook.'

'I'll buy you a book. There are some excellent ones around, I believe.'

With a snort of laughter she pressed a kiss to his chin. 'You can *buy* it, but...'

'Good job I'm wealthy,' Tano observed mournfully. 'Looks like we'll be eating out rather a lot.'

'*You* could learn... Will you mind?' she asked softly. 'Really?'

'What do you think?' he asked, with a delightfully loving smile. 'But it might be as well to at least learn to boil milk; I don't think I would like our children to go hungry.'

'You mean any children of yours won't be *born* coping?'

'Now, now,' he reproved her. 'Underneath this tough exterior is a very vulnerable man.'

'Rubbish!' she snorted. 'No,' she denied, 'not rubbish—or not entirely. Everyone is vulnerable to some degree or another. Sorry, I didn't mean... Oh, shut up.'

'I didn't say a word!'

'You didn't have to!' Idly smoothing non-existent hairs on his chest, her eyes on her very pleasurable task, she began tentatively, 'Tano?'

'Mmm.'

'Are you smiling?'

'A little; amused by your sudden meekness, perhaps.'

Raising her head, Rea smiled at him. 'I can be meek...'

'I know. And loving. Go on, what were you going to ask?'

'Only about social circles. No, don't groan. I mean—'

'Will you be ostracised because you're an English peasant?' he asked, tongue-in-cheek.

'I'm not a peasant! And let me tell you I'm as good as any of your fancy nobles...' Seeing his grin, she slapped him playfully. 'What were your parents like?'

'Noble. No,' he denied, with a smile. 'I don't really know what my father was like, but everyone says he was like me. And my mother was a darling.'

'Were you very close?'

'Yes. She was a delightful lady. Forceful.' He grinned. 'Decidedly autocratic.'

'But with a heart of gold,' she added firmly.

'Of course. Is there any doubt? You think I could love you if I didn't think that?'

'We weren't talking about me.'

'Weren't we?' he asked gently.

Raising her head again, Rea confessed, 'Maybe— a little. It's just that you haven't seen a very good side of me so far and I wanted you to know that I can be—nice.'

'I know. Can you also learn Italian?'

'Of course.' Moving into a more comfortable position, she rested her elbows on his chest, grinned unrepentantly when he grunted, and proffered loftily, 'I could maybe even learn about archaeology, or take coach tours, become an obelisk expert.'

'Do I detect a note of mockery in your tone, Miss Halton?'

'Quite possibly—but not about loving you,' she promised gently.

'No,' he agreed as he removed her elbows, snuggled her warmly into his arms. 'Never about loving me.'

'I'll even be quite nice to Angélique,' she promised rashly, and he grunted. 'I will. I can be magnanimous. But—'

'There isn't any need for buts. You have my solemn word.'

She nodded, comforted, and he whispered something, his mouth almost touching hers—a tantalising delight that made her wriggle against him—and then he explained, 'That was your first Italian lesson. It means "I love you".'

'I know,' she agreed, softly smug. 'That much I do know. I looked it up.'

'Then say it.'

'I love you.'

'In *Italian*, you fool.'

'No. You'll laugh at my accent.'

Tano laughed anyway, in utter delight, and then began to teach her a lot of other nice things. Or Rea taught him. In a partnership teaching was—reciprocal.

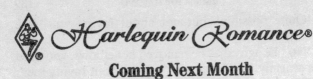

Harlequin Romance®

Coming Next Month

#3431 BRINGING UP BABIES Emma Goldrick
Holding Out for a Hero
Hope Latimore had taken a job as a stand-in nanny before she realized
her new boss was Ralph Browne, the man who had made her high
school days hell! Unfortunately, she was stuck with him—she couldn't
leave Eddie and little Melody with a bachelor dad to contend with.
Sexy, Ralph might be, but it was clear he knew less than Hope about
bringing up kids!

#3432 THE COWBOY WANTS A WIFE! Susan Fox
Hitched!
She's a glamorous Hollywood socialite, he's a tough, rugged
rancher.... They're worlds apart, but could it be that Zoe is just
the wife for John Dalton Hayes—even though the very last thing he
wants to do is marry?

#3433 TEMPORARY HUSBAND Day Leclaire
Fairytale Weddings
Harlequin Romance invites you to a wedding...
                    ...And it could be your own!
On one very special night, single people from all over America come
together in the hope of finding that special ingredient for a happy-
ever-after—their soul mate. The inspiration behind The Cinderella
Ball is simple—come single, leave wed. Which is exactly what happens
to three unsuspecting couples in Day Leclaire's great new trilogy....

Wynne Sommers needs a husband. She wants a guy who is tall, strong
and fearless. She gets Jake Hondo! He's a mean, moody rancher who
needs to get married, on paper at least, to secure his own estate.
Wynne isn't his idea of a temporary wife...for starters she has an
inheritance of her own...kids!

#3434 DREAM WEDDING Helen Brooks
When Reece employed Miriam to organize a dream wedding for his
sister, he never expected to be making marriage plans of his own. But
Miriam could be about to change his mind!

AVAILABLE THIS MONTH:

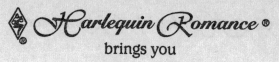

Harlequin Romance ®

brings you

How the West was Wooed!

We've rounded up twelve of our most popular authors, and the result is a whole year of romance, Western-style. Every month we'll be bringing you a spirited, independent woman whose heart is about to be lassoed by a rugged, handsome, one-hundred-percent cowboy!

Watch for...

brings you

Some men are worth waiting for!

Every month for a whole year Harlequin Romance will be bringing you some of the world's most eligible men in our special **Holding Out for a Hero** miniseries.

They're handsome, they're charming but, best of all, they're single! Twelve lucky women are about to discover that finding Mr. Right is not a problem—it's holding on to him!

Watch for:

#3431 BRINGING UP BABIES
by Emma Goldrick

Available in November wherever Harlequin books are sold.